OPPOSITE OF SHADOW

BRIAN BENDLIN & LINDA SMITH

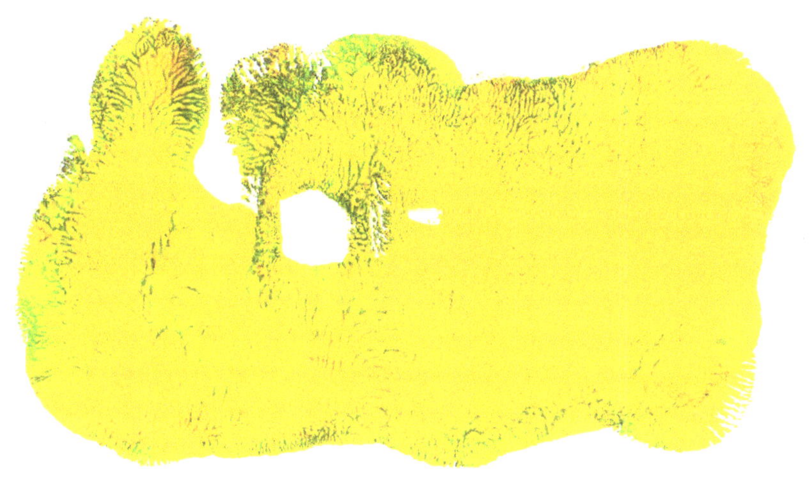

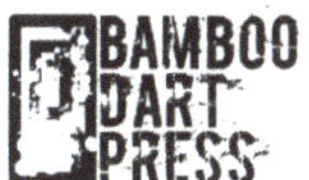

LOS ANGELES † NEW YORK † LONDON † MELBOURNE

Opposite of Shadow by Brian Bendlin & Linda Smith

ISBN: 978-1-947240-86-5

First Printing 2023

Artwork by Linda Smith

Writing by Brian Bendlin

Editing by Dennis Callaci

Layout and design by Mark Givens and Linda Smith

To access *13 Groves* by Brian Bendlin, please visit
http://www.bamboodartpress.com/music/brian_bendlin-13_groves.html

For information:
Bamboo Dart Press
chapbooks@bamboodartpress.com

Bamboo Dart Press Special Projects 003

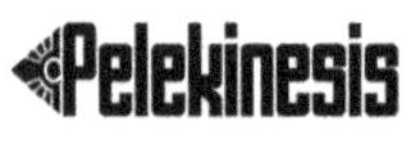

www.pelekinesis.com

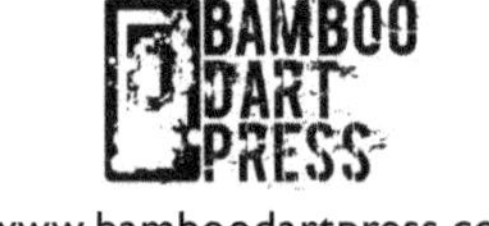

www.bamboodartpress.com

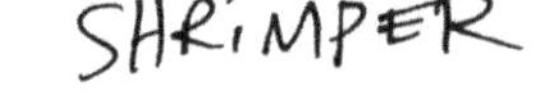

www.shrimperrecords.com

CONTENTS

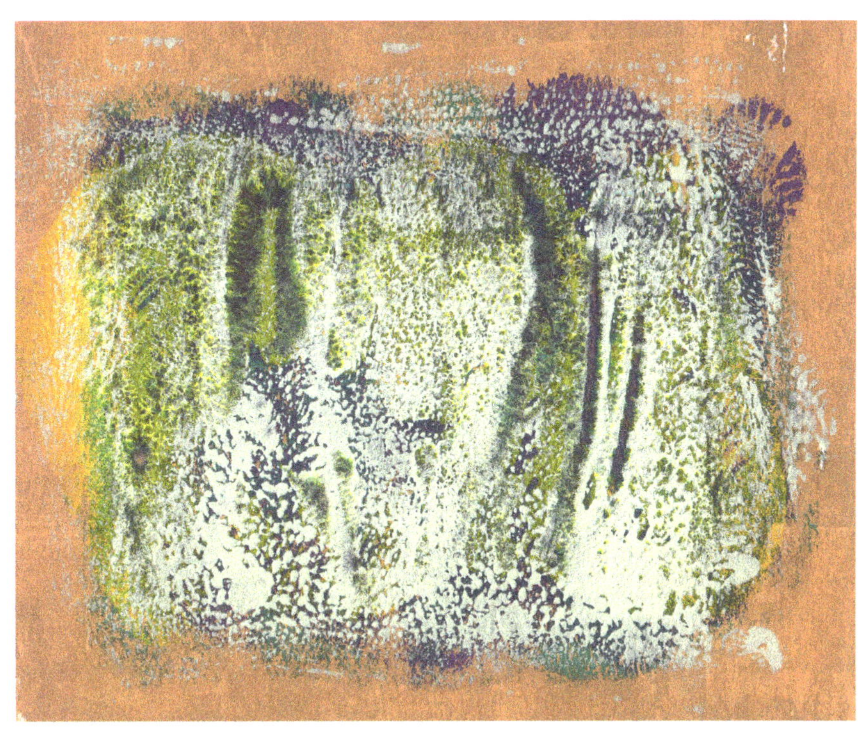

Map

I wanted to speak to what is here, but could not because of what is missing. Instead I will write the absence, what has left.

Verona to Spring Green, 1978

So I will write the absence, and only what is left   here and from a long way back   from other towns   lakes and rivers late slant of summer   light on the side of the road   woods in a certain countryside   a naked quarry   the log rolls in water and the rope swings.

The removal of simple things: watch   shoes before clothes so much water pushed through the hand   stand on a sandbar swim against the river's pull.   Warm pools off the peninsula in the cold lake   the juice of the bruised melons thieved from a field as the light fades.

The broken vent on the old car, the cold air.   *Go.*   *There.* And there, even so   no need for the blanket.   A presumption of sunrise,   still, and   still awake at dawn, guard down   and because we can we   watch another sleep   (how it is that one lies long in bed, cannot be called tall)   awaken in a strange place late in the day.

Gifts not given on days not holidays: a hundred-year-old book of fantasy   wool for denim   jacket for sweater, exchanged of scent   sampled in a medicine bottle that bore his name.

And though the railroad said   *travel*   *go ahead*   *there*   rode up instead on a motorcycle   to utter the only thing left: I came to see my friend.

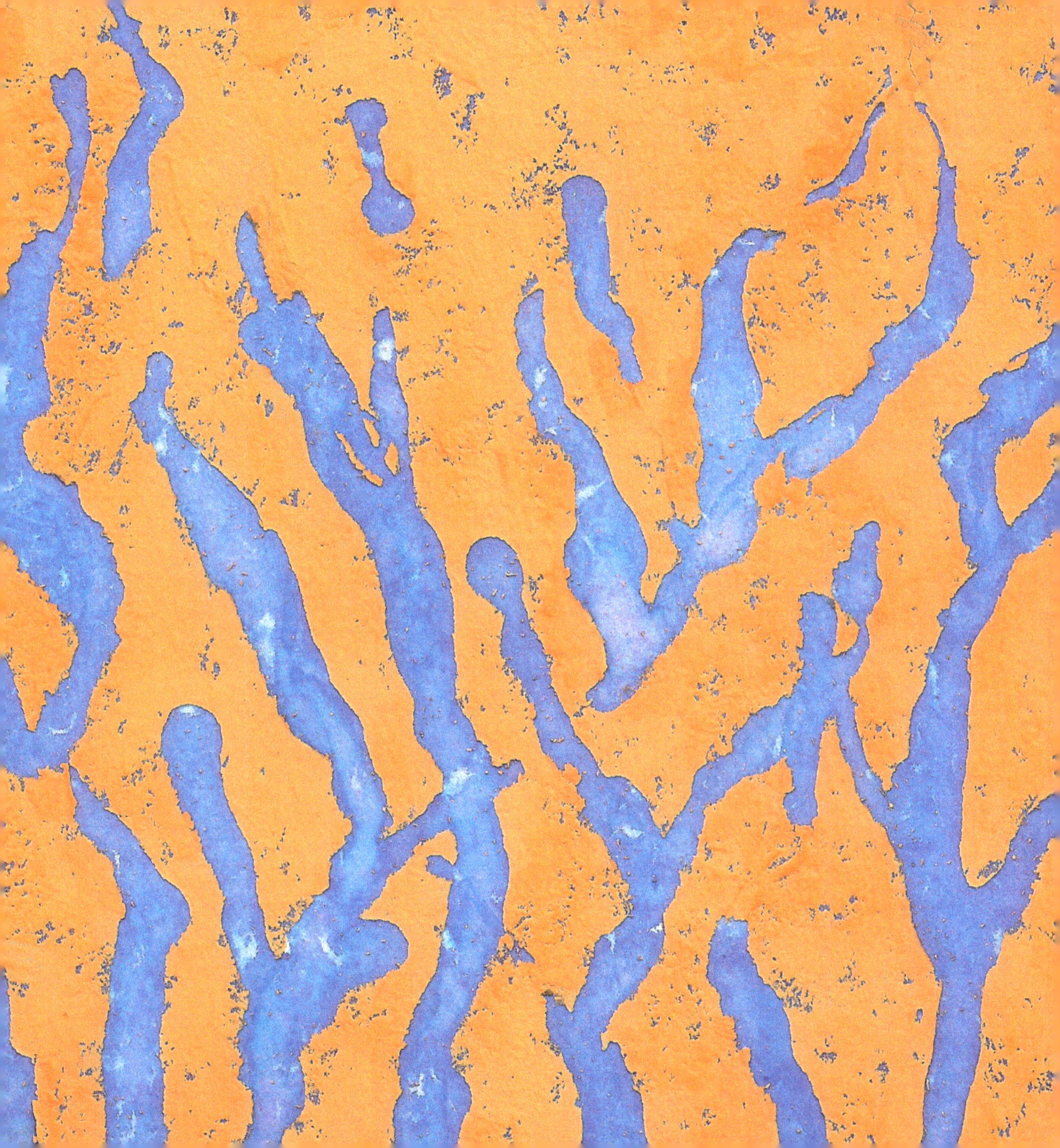

Lake Mendota, 1979

This is how we: some suspense   if it happens happens slowly submerged not waist first   dust, dusk, dog barks, cries from the cobbled street   tension in humid August air.   The light dims, but he hasn't turned on a light.   The misnamed northern Casa Rita   the last of the sun on terra-cotta.

Buchanan, 1993

You might have made sense of all this.   Listen: There it should be green (if it is as I first saw it)   an old house of antiques, brocade   bridge over the James   a rusted fence the railroad passing and of the past.   It is cool and damp, muddy near the daffodils.

Here instead is the smell of fresh paint   the crowded boxes of moving in, dust of moving out.   The smell of bags of lightly roasted coffee   carried north from a Florida supermarket, wrapped in Spanish moss thieved from the trees.   In summer the view west to the river   a falling sun and the quiet of seven. In winter these bare trees in cold sky.   Here a map settles arguments: *this* is the island and *that* is the beach.   Here, in aperitif, the bitter lingering.   The esses we ran our fingers in between handclaps   and the laugh of the last good night.

Star Route 1, Ely, 1979

The sun   in a fall   shadow over, on   a bluff   above and crossing boundary waters.   Wanted, perfect, profound   :this as close to   :no other moment in life may ever seem so.

Buttocks Island, 1995

Sight and site returned   the hillock over the river   for some clue of what was once: a broken blue wine glass   brand name on a cigarette butt   a sign posted   letter written with the important final message.   The limb of a suicide: said *scar* right index finger across left forearm   *scar*, *scar*, *scar*, *scar*. The stray hairs on a leg like cracked clay in the desert.   The crack on the wall   or a leak or a bug in the old house.   Flat spaces and cold air   :this is what remains in his unhappy room but now it need be more.

Lake Mendota to Lake Monona, 1981

Once, snuck in summer   behind the fraternity house   only two of us among the five there   jumping   jutted limb unashamed   under, into water.

The second earlier   in winter   to the bar in the basement of the old hotel.   We made our way across the frozen lake skating, then stopping   to drunkenly sweep angels from the snow.

Phoenicia, 1993

It was not as I remembered it.   The meadow was overgrown there were no vestiges of the campfire.   The creek had dried up, and so I could not swim.

Strange to think   it could be anything but memory   lichened to a rock at the edge of the sere creek.   The remembered howl of the wild dog, the first across the meadow   or the second the moon rose over the mountain   frightened first shadow.

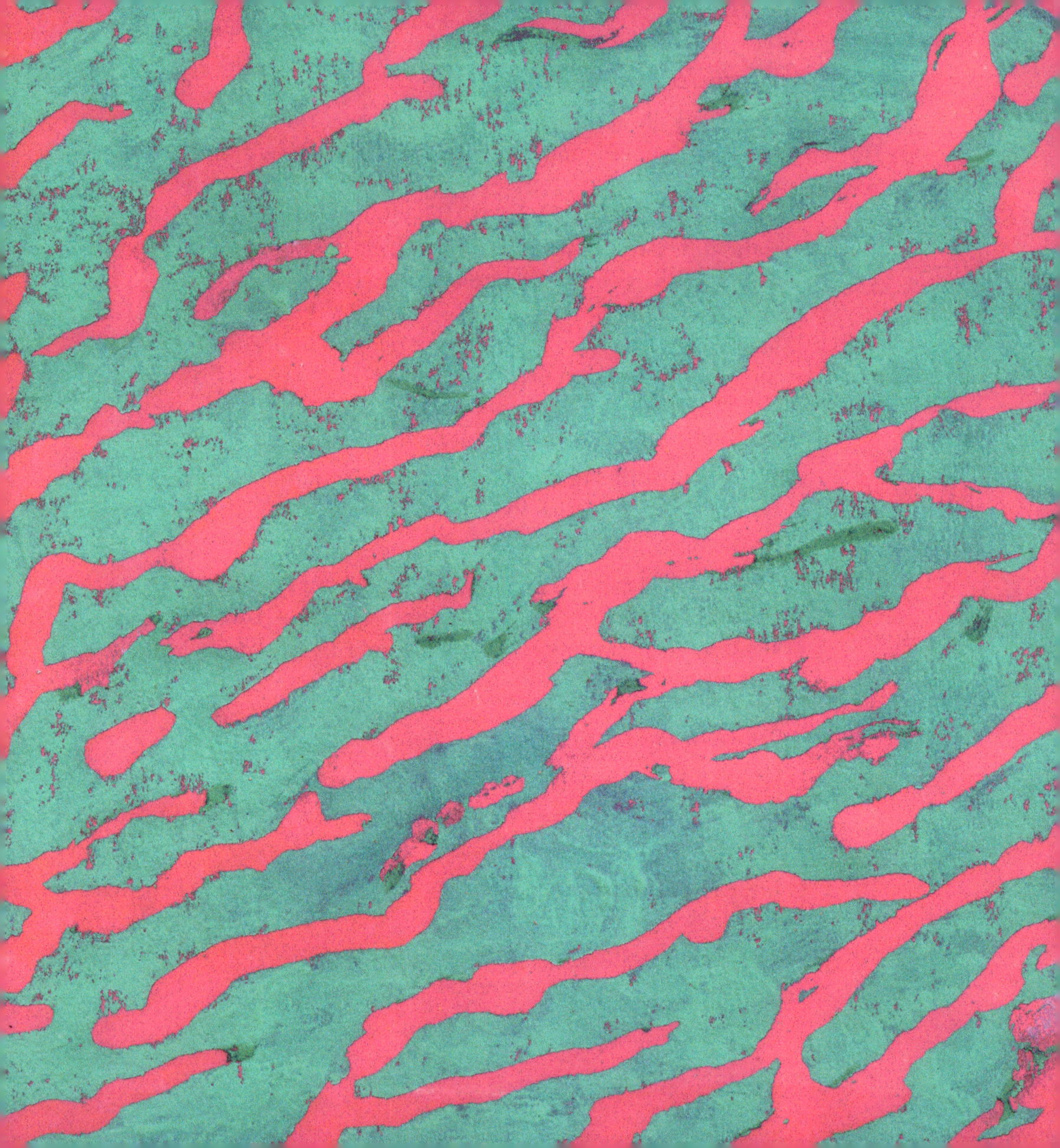

Sawkill to Ward Manor, 1993

Reading on the manor lawn, in the sun, I fell asleep. Something, some thought   of napping on the spare bed. (There, sheltered and congenial   there a photograph with a woman,   a map of the past.)   Seeing, waking me: something in that too.   Substances as enticements: the trappings of adulthood   what we could not have when we were younger. As bare as only a friendship be   and maybe only that.

Rokeby Farm, 1994

At night the river is not seen   water, body   cast only by a single light   high on the old wood post   or shadow of the mansion glow   a stranger.   Drunken grin   against a veranda column.   Not here to see the books in the octagonal library but to follow the flash of shirt, blond tress.   The wood is old. It might give way.   The expensive china on the side table may be knocked over and broken.

Everything desired   right now is simple, uncomplicated.   Call it naive and take advantage.   Return to it   if and when invited.

Dingman's Ferry, 1992

The break of faith and fall of water   well, they can't be helped. Grinning under the river   bridge in the rain   cans of cheap local beer   a ball to the river for the dog.

Although it rained, the day was perfect.   Think: I've been here before, this place.   It is always awkward yet somehow pleasant.

Phantom Lake to Devil's Lake, Jasonville to Sun Prairie, 1976

As if to dredge him from the river you appear, flat in the sun on a wooden dock.   If I asked you to speak, would you be in his tongue?   Would you bring ash from the cone of the volcano   sweep it from his shoulders and his garden soil   dip his foot in night water at Devil's Lake?

Walking   the first leg ignorant and innocent   across the February ice   roof over Phantom Lake.   The next leg brushed   that was once all and enough.

The squeak of an old bed   betrayal balanced on a fallen limb   brood in a tree on the shore of a lake in Indiana   salt sweat in a sleeping bag   straw hat, stripped trunk in a rocking chair.

Two years later   and the roses are blooming along the river   in some form of allure   on the edge of the bed as if to say *now it is right, but now it is too late.*

No last leg   the wrong food, a red herring.   Apology and attraction   what could never be said as the road wound south-west in the cornfield rain   or lay across a field of sunflowers.

Sawkill, 1992

Remember this, then: the young man in the waterfall.   The color of clothes when he departs   the path he takes through the woods.   The large white car.   How he reappears later behind a building in the trees.   That intuition can only be intuition   only   so many things can be guessed when not really knowing   longing as espionage.   How the map is read   spread out and leaning   on the car's white hood.   You will talk about it   and return again.   And again.

Elm Grove to South Milwaukee, 1976

Fake   passes in the night.   Skin against the glass of the sliding door   the smell of the cork wall.   Offerings: the white gauze shirt, sloe gin fizz, spit   the railroad coat.   A broken kite on the cliff over Lake Michigan.   Faces in old photographs.

Blackwater River to Alabama, 1999

The farther south   farther away   those first of ten days   the more I eased   the car over mountains   back roads   bought the cheapest gasoline, bourbon, cigarettes.   Country music on the radio   station leaving range   another to fade in and replace it.

The more alone the more I was   myself content   to walk, to drive the sand   the strand of highway parallel to the gulf.

In the afternoon heat I started back   through bayous   gators, turtles   sand, slash, shortleaf, longleaf, pond pines   through small towns, main streets lined with palms.   Night rolled down the window   and for hours the scent of Confederate jasmine.

At every crossroads pulled Cantonment   another highway same road, different road, same number   called back, pulled to black water   a turtle sunned on a log.

Picnic Point, 1978

Careful, quiet on the floor   he could not   have not   known the arc of that night.   The next day   then   hands and arms, other friends   the sun   a small meadow on the peninsula.

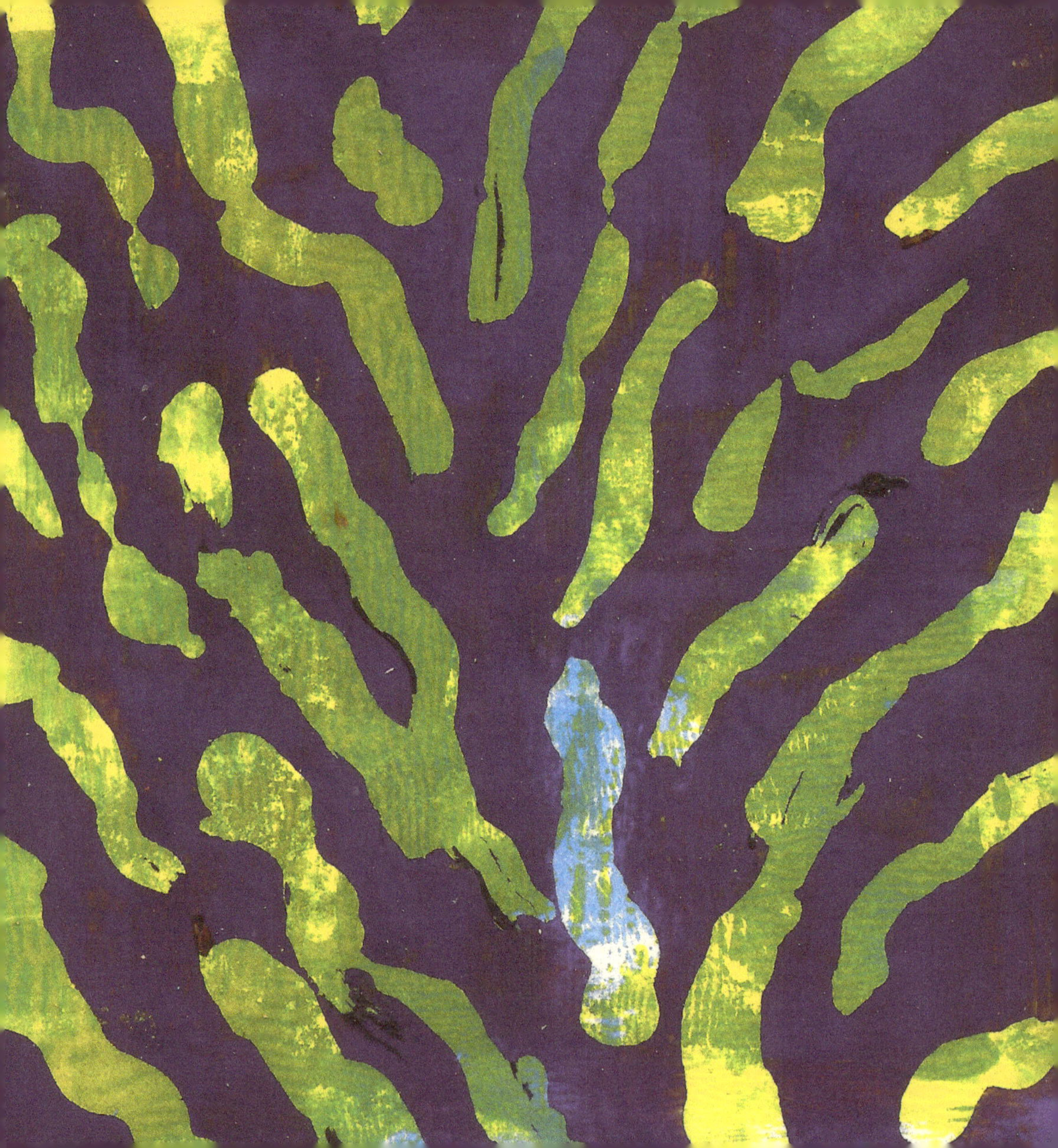

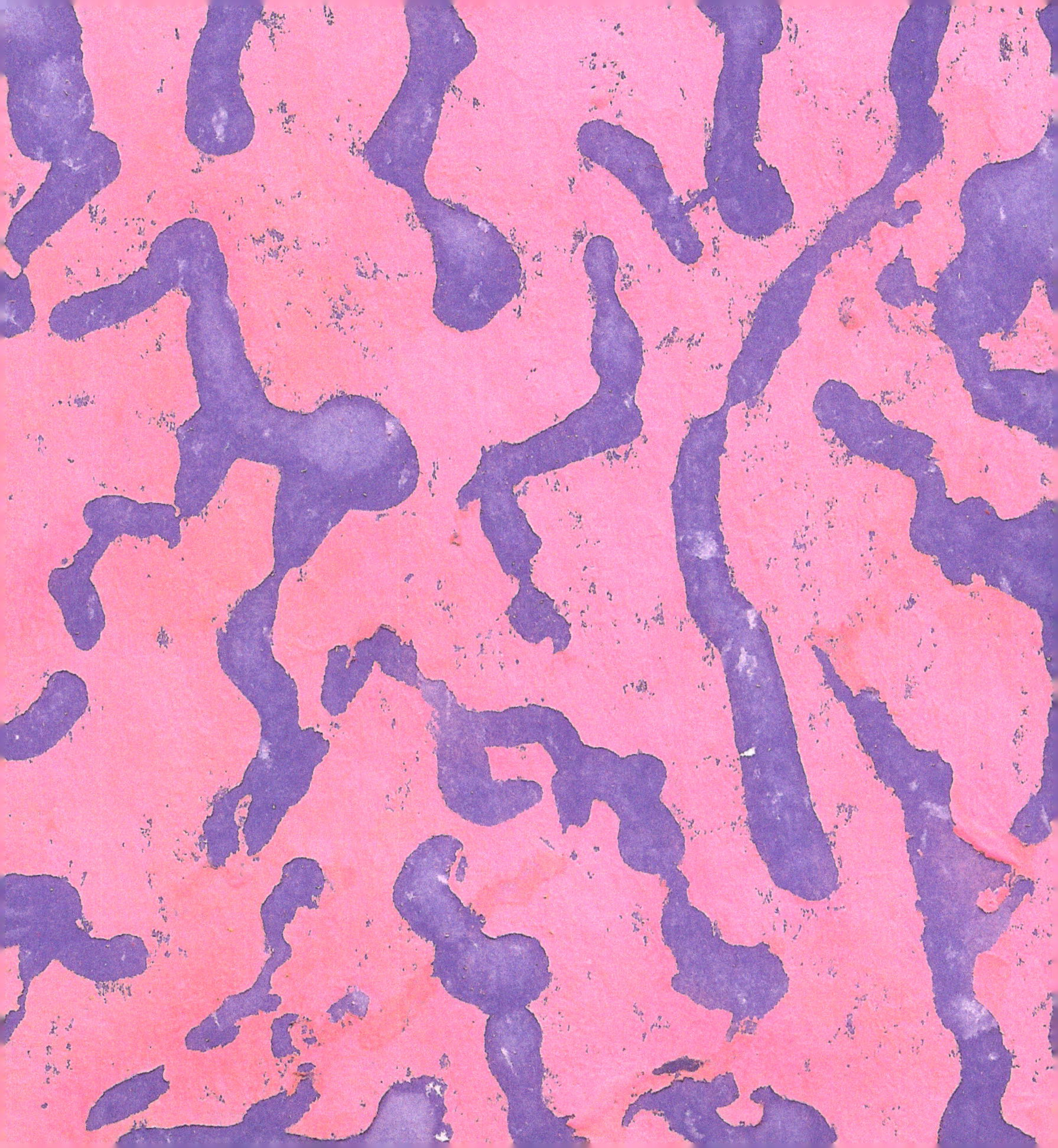

Brookfield Quarry to Lake Minnewaska to Black's Beach, time unspecified

Famous crumbcake cliffs.   To be lost here   but found diving from the rocks   rolling in the thick mud in the shallows.   See, there is the invitation card: Bring nothing.   Men scaled the stony drops   like mountain goats   and I have the sandy cliffs two thousand miles away.   Here is the shift change: those who sun on the flat rocks and swim by day   now those who swim at night, when it is silent but for the frogs.   And all of it fabricated   all of it a lie.

Sawkill, 1995

If they asked you what effect your appearance might have had, you could tell them for me: body   of water   trim, tanned, twigged hut   the bare rhythmed steps over a circle of fire walk on mossed rocks   a thin beard sculpted from question marks.

You could tell them   how all of this leads loss, brings back the mistakes made years ago   pulls longing out from under the skin of the simple embrace   that might give   like so many others   if one knew you better (as others have).

And tell the fear of the next step   and how this never changed. How everything that has happened is a question from an archive of questions   and what is written in the books is only more of them: how you   how they   turned out   where they ended up, where it ends.   Assign names to them: some would still be anonymous   nameless point, an X on a map to treasure what has been left behind, lost   stolen or forgotten.

Resonance and echoes and smoke demand their time   do not

want to fall or be lost. A life recorded and played back. How one might vow to never grow old, or work, or wear clothes laid bare only matter if someone is there to see it.

And you could explain what happens to the lump of hope, the pile of want where it goes when it sinks what is missing: phantom pain, reason, balm. Then I can tell you about what is here.

Once that is said, then maybe I can tell you about what is here: The dog's wagging tail on the rutted road in a field of tall grass; the vinca and daylilies, things escaped from cultivation. How each flicker of leaf could be the chrome of a bicycle, the white shirt, the white car, a dart of skin submerging. How the air might smell some day.

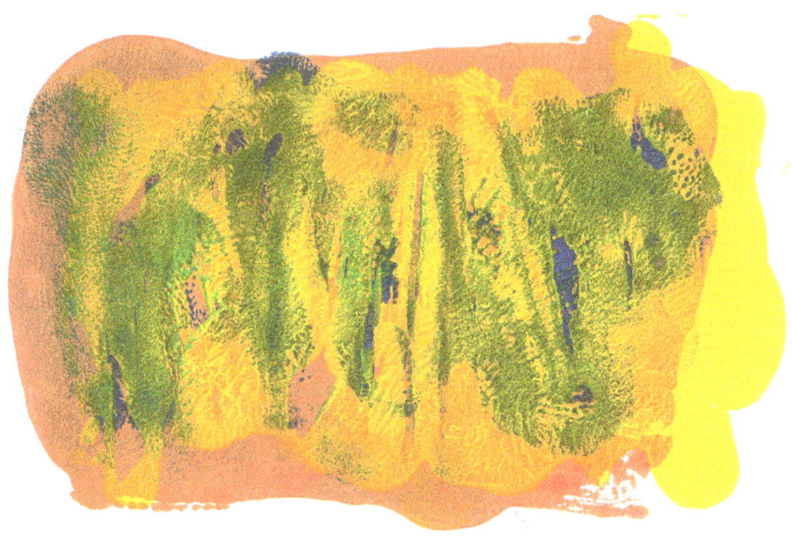

Rain Three

A letter about the sun   spoke hot held heat: Burn on the sand   said   on the pavement.   Sun on the lawns.

Tonight could write rain everywhere, sing a year's flood song. If this crumble of cloud continued to hurl itself   could sleep sleep through it   fields contain it?   Ground hold hard   or drain   or swamp   or rivers flood   wood waterlogged?

If bowel of sky   dog gray   and a bellows rose noise   orange sky stayed   striation   how a life could change   never lit again beyond lightning.   And everything then be water.

Tonight could write rain everywhere   speak water, write wet: Flood on the grass   say   on the pavement.   Mud on the lawns.

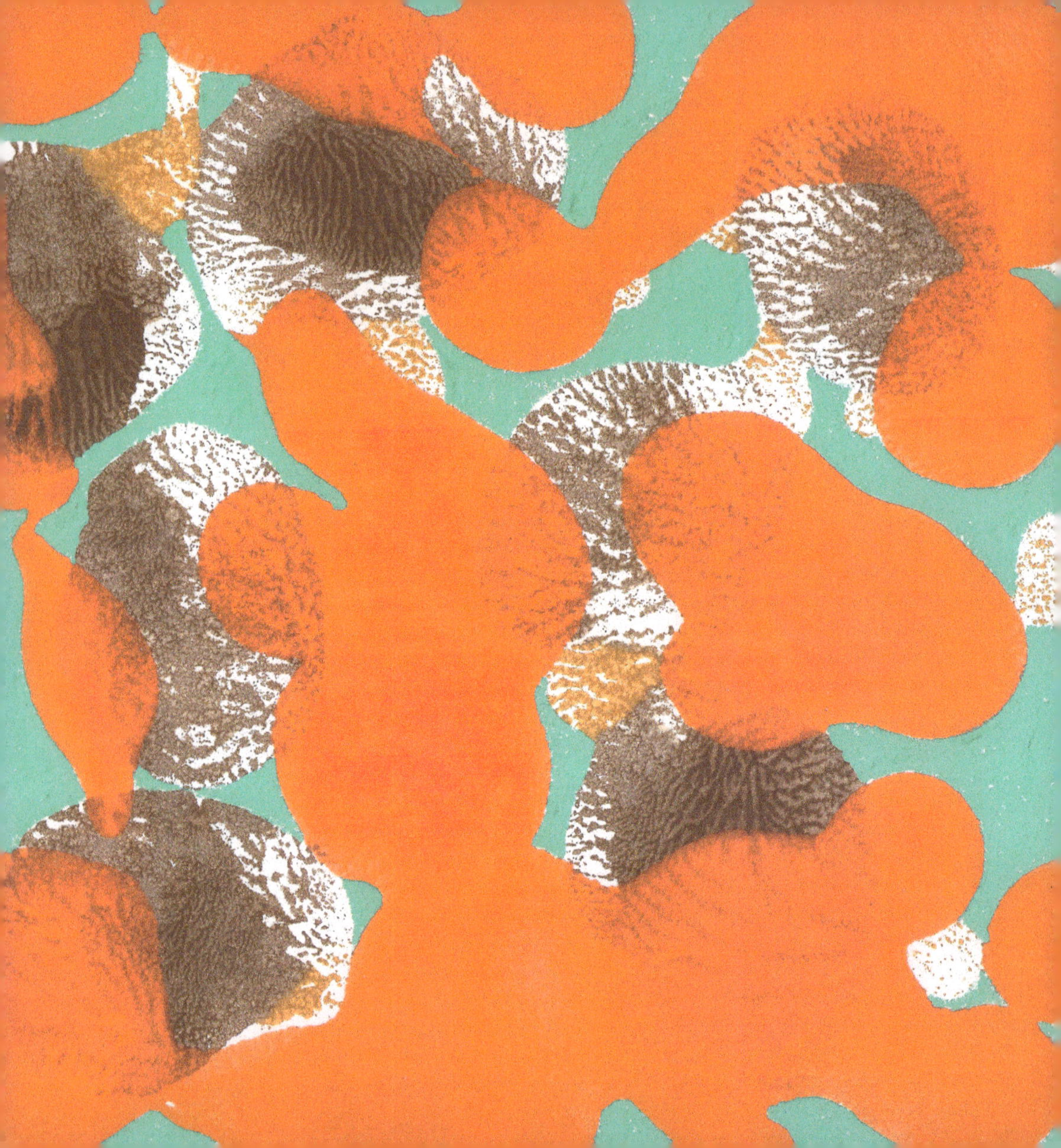

Birds

Earlier saw a summer storm   split trees with lightning   move wind in a graying, sideways rain   move   plastic carts across the parking lot's black tar.   And feathered birds: What pulled them, what   unstaggered magnet, slow methodic   could draw them to this station?

Famous birds.   Down, across   to fuel their patience   wait for wind to say the word: Attack.

Everything is new here.

Ailanthus

Ailanthus altissima; also Chinese Sumac, tree of paradise. Confused often with the sumac, from which it may be distinguished by the male ailanthus tree's rank, unpleasant odor.

From many places they bring the names vegetation there: oak, elm, crimson maple, white underwind on poplar leaves.

It is then to turn up what is known from the ground here, grown wild: weed tree. And after many years lent learned names.

One night thought she smelled sour tomcat spray another, sweet flowers. One day thought he liked the way it grew on rooftops.

From cities turned found a way at the roadside ailanthus in a native bed.

Head away now they who come from cities tire of tree of paradise, try to remember another: What is the name of this bush I've known since childhood sweet smell afar from the hedged end of Florida motel sidewalk then and weak, white, foul-bitter flowers close up?

It lives here too, now.

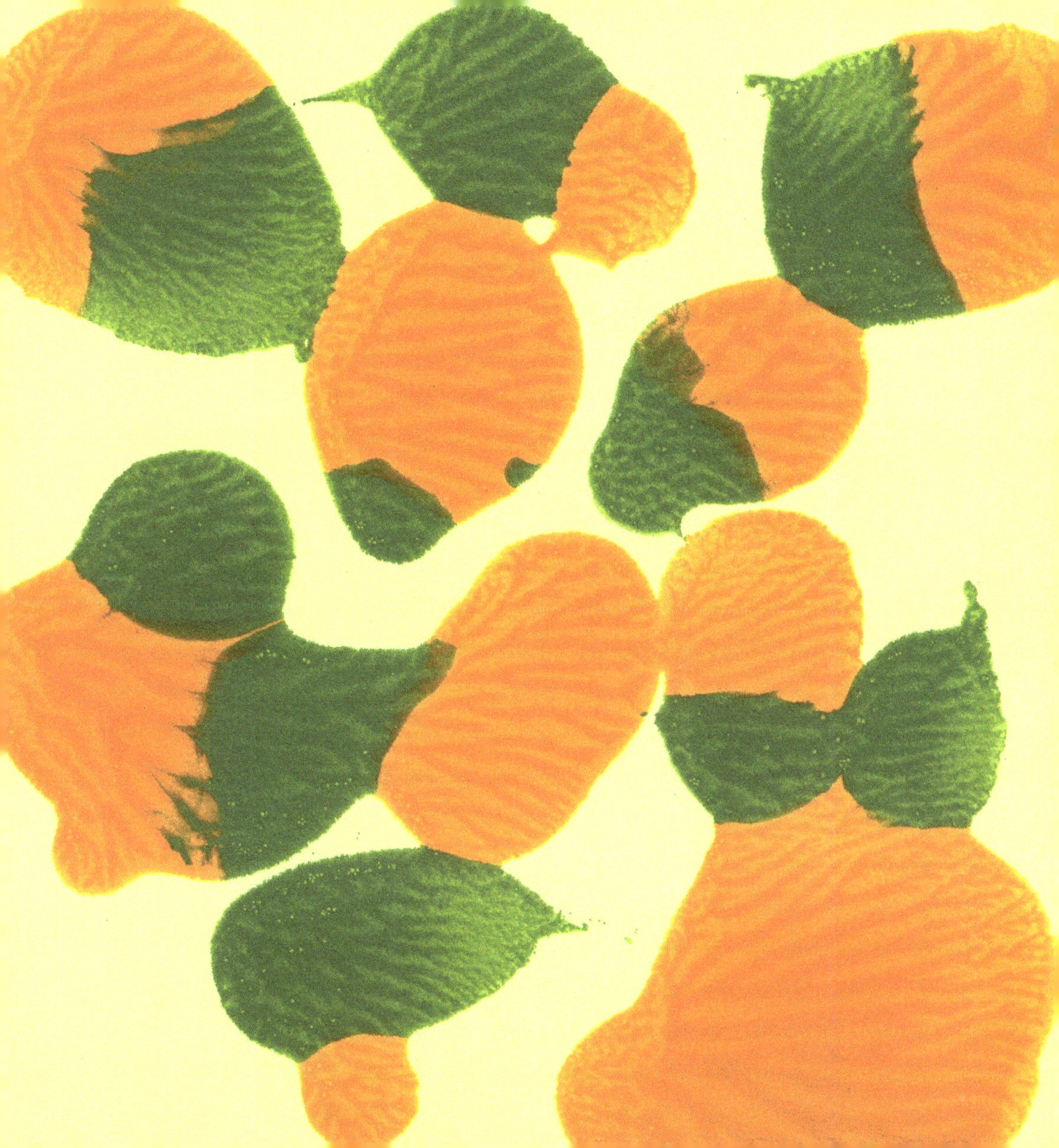

Manse

1

Once a house for the wealthy   once for the aged   once   for the insane (or so they say),   now they come to stay here spend hours at the dim of day   on wine   deer and woodchuck, bat, fox, firefly.

And one knows: yes   those mountains were here and just as high   when this house was built   back some hundred years above a field   back away from the river   and that is why it was built west.   But what about those trees   that one, and that one there   were they here   as tall?

Once they could see the river from this house.

2

In this   a fine room   and dark   wood wound(ed) now by years   of neglect, the wrong   furniture   now guard, now preserve:

Do not sing, drink a round   around the dark table, dance   on these oak floors. Remove   the old chairs   bring back the older   oil   the wood, these walls.   Rehang the chandeliers and do not rend this fabric.   Do not tear.

3

The things that are not scene   but to know what has been   is there: red light on mountain, under nimbus at dark   (dis) comfort.

The train heard at night   one remembers too   from Buchanan, Virginia   :that is how it is said.

4

Once inside   in separated rooms   hymns: canticle from the eaves of the older house   again   from windows in the new from the slate floors   the whistle of old   pipes in the walls the hum of a truck that passes.   Even the mockingbird cants it still.

Until it is no longer sung from radio or room   but the stone itself   the air   the manor lit   a canon.

5

Notice: planes at the horizons   notice : strata   curved line of mountain mirrored   by line of trees   deep shade   mirrored at the edge of   and field meets grass.   Longer there, then shorter   deeper   shade of nile or jade.

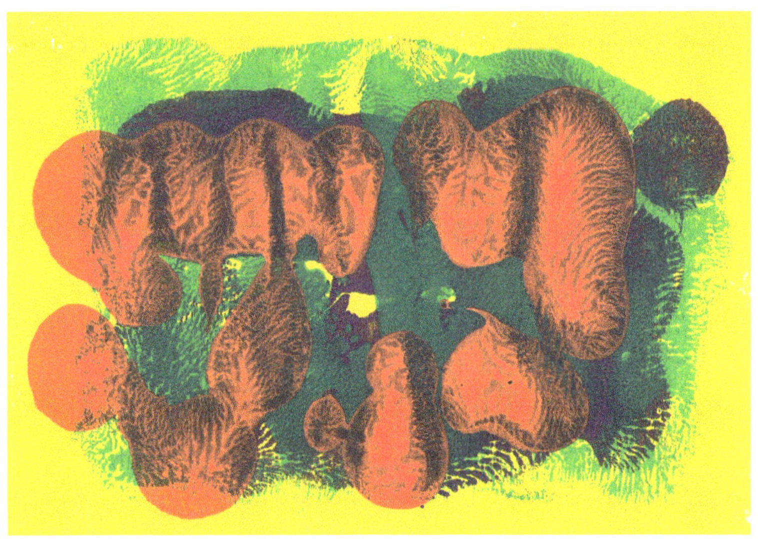

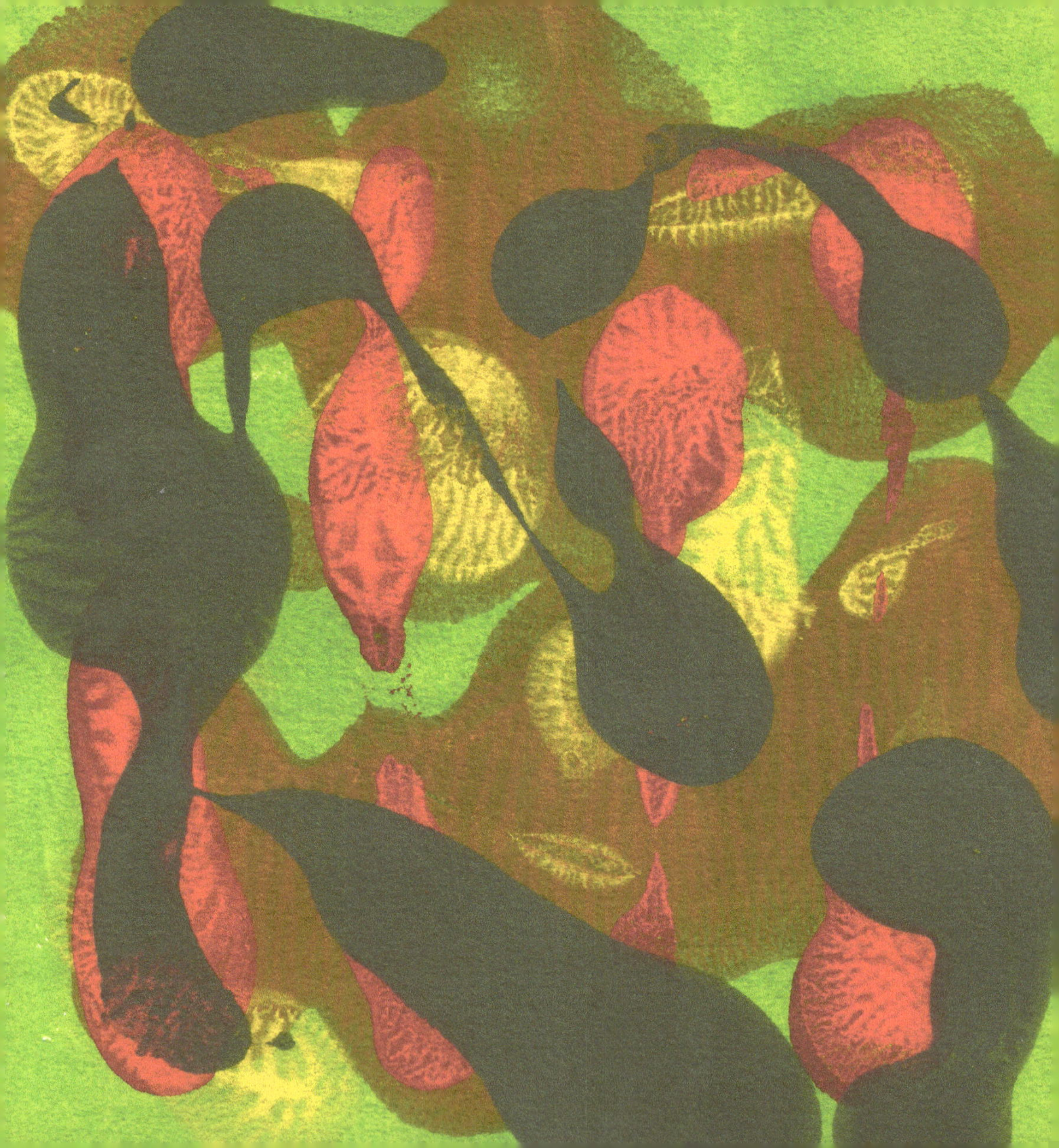

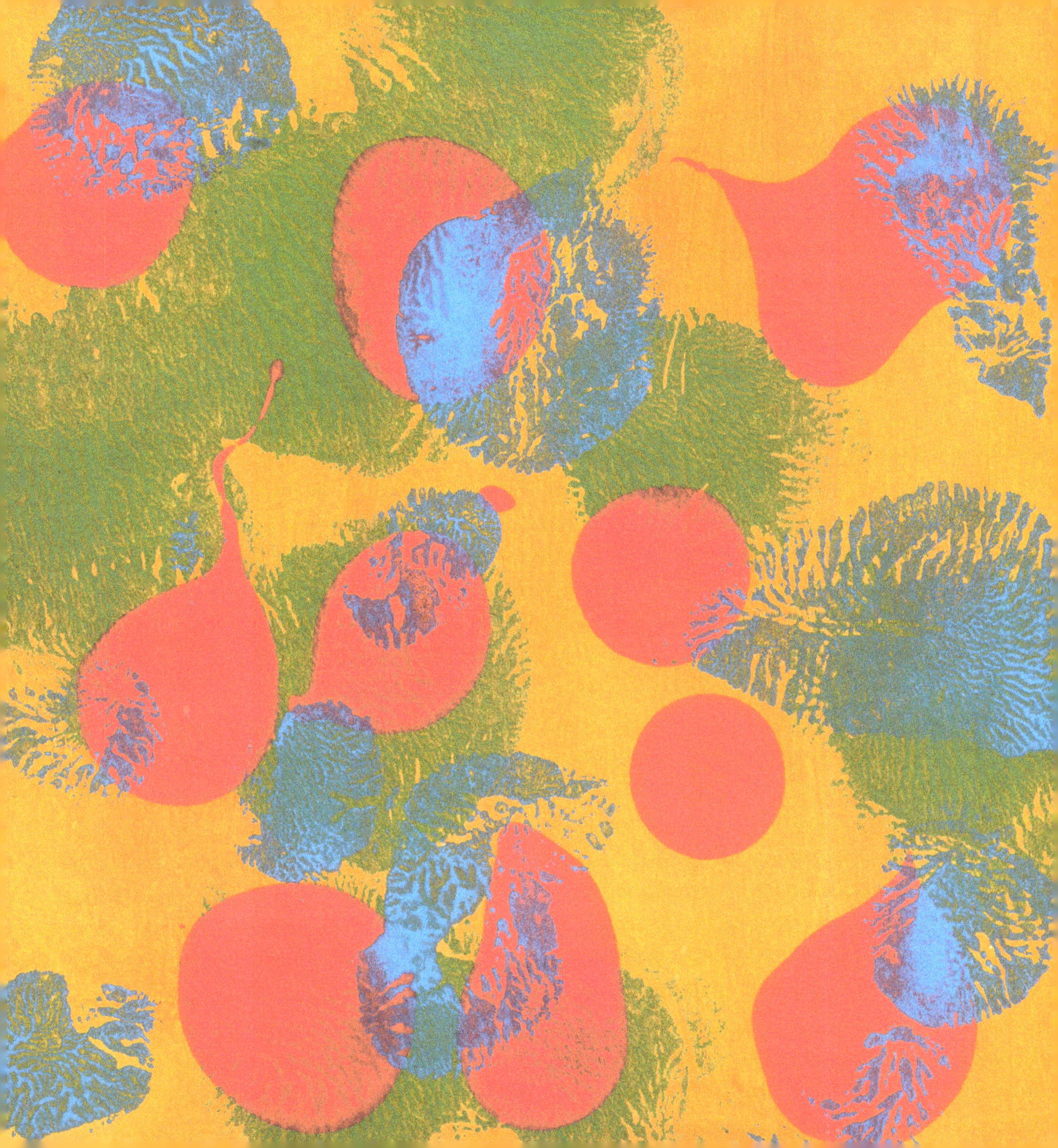

Up Here

Part One: A Road to Something

I live in the country now. For years, when I lived in cities, I went places to experience them. Now I need only sit or stand in place to see what comes to me.

On this early October night it is the mouse that has come in from the cold to perch on the bathroom's shower caddy. We have tried scaring it, which only caused it to frantically tightrope-walk the shower curtain rod. We ignored it during dinner by shutting the bathroom door in hopes that it might go back into whatever hole it first came through, but now I have returned to the bathroom, only to find the corner of a bar of soap gnawed away and the mouse still there. The cats have not seen it, and I would let them have at it if I didn't think a loud fight would come between them. And a cat can't walk across a shower curtain rod anyway.

So now we have come to the most elaborate of schemes, a series of wood plank ramps that lead from the shower curtain rod to the window frame, and from the window to the seat of the riding lawnmower parked behind the house. To entice the mouse, corn chips are laid along the planks at three-inch intervals. It works, and once the mouse is outside we abruptly knock the last ramp loose and slam the window shut, but then are ridden with guilt for having sent the mouse out into the cold. This is, of course, ridiculous, because it will only return another night to meet the cats.

What came to us tonight could as easily have been the weird albino bug that stopped by this afternoon, perched behind a bottle on the bathroom shelf, its eyes shifting, magnified by the bottle's oil and through the glass.

What came to us tonight could just as easily have been the butterfly that came yesterday evening, immobile on the grass outside the back door. We picked it up and brought it in the house, gently setting it inside a china cabinet to keep it from the cats. Later in the evening, deciding it was cold, we placed it on the fireplace mantel, and within an hour it showed more signs of life, crawling across a branch of bittersweet there, moving its wings only when one or the other of us spoke. We left it there at the end of the night, and this morning I found it on the living room rug, its wings perforated by cat claws. It moved just slightly as I threw it into the embers of last night's fire, where it sizzled briefly and then was gone.

It is almost Halloween, and the holiday takes its form on the local houses and in the yards.

North of here, on the county highway, there is a farmhouse and, in front of it, two mailboxes. One is a galvanized steel box, standing at the regulation forty-one inches or so above the ground on a wooden post. The other, a similar box, stands on a steel pole that stretches some fifteen feet into the air; painted on the side of it are the words AIR MAIL.

But that is not the joke—or, at least, not a new one. I have seen that before, a lifetime ago, in the midwestern suburb where I grew up. Instead the joke appeared later in the month, when, near these mailboxes, white cotton ghosts appeared in the trees, hung by their necks with rope nooses. A large hay wagon was parked by the road, surrounded by jack-o'-lanterns, and atop the wagon—propped up by bales of hay—was an open wooden coffin, oblique and hexagonal, Dracula style, containing a skeleton. On the side of the coffin hung a sign that read THE DEATH OF ANOTHER CIGARETTE SMOKER.

South of here, on another highway, there is a large farm market that has set out a display of many lit jack-o'-lanterns on the roadside, half facing north and half south, two rows each. The effect is dazzling: driving that road tonight I noticed, from a half mile away, the construct of orange light. It wasn't until my car neared the farm that I could see that each of the large pumpkins had a letter carved into it and that they spelled not HAPPY HALLOWEEN but VOTE REPUBLICAN.

❖

It is late November, and tonight I sat outside as long as I could, as it was an unusually warm day. I was listening to the cows, deep in the valley at the dairy farm, and to the geese in the cornfield just above them.

Just before sunset, geese flew over in small groups, V formations. Each group circled once or twice before landing in the field, where the feed corn had recently been harvested and stray ears and kernels lay scattered for a meal. At first it was just a few of them; then another group, and then another and another, until the field, at least a square mile in area, was black with birds. I counted the number of geese in one small patch, then did my best to multiply that area according to the whole expanse of the cornfield. There were, I figured, well over two thousand geese. Earlier a friend called on the telephone, and we tried to speak, but the honking of the two thousand could even be heard inside the house. The din was extraordinary; she could hardly hear me speak, and by necessity the call was cut short.

The electricity went out soon after sunset when a truck hit a power pole. I could see it, first: a bright flash from the highway in the valley below. Then, a few seconds later, the delayed sound of the collision as it traveled up the hill to the house, then sudden quiet and total darkness once the outage made its way up the wires. The force with which power returned later—every kitchen appliance abruptly buzzing, humming, or flashing, the radio suddenly blaring electricity—was as jarring as its earlier disappearance.

Inside, the fire, dry oak, smells like nutmeg, in odd contrast to the oak logs stacked on the back porch, damp and musty, vomit-sour. The cats lie so close to the flames that their fur is too hot to touch when I try to move them. I picture a cat suddenly in flames: the spontaneous combustion that supposedly happens to some unfortunate souls, as one reads about in supermarket tabloids.

The cats are content in their roles, having killed two mice earlier in the week. The first I found in the hallway, its stomach opened, entrails splayed across the floor; the other lay on the living room rug, whole of body but decapitated, its head nowhere to be found. That same night, reaching into the dark of the kitchen sink's drain, I felt a mushy, furry ball thing, and I recoiled, presuming it to be a mouse head deposited by a cat, but it turned out to be the rehydrated seed head of one of the wildflowers I

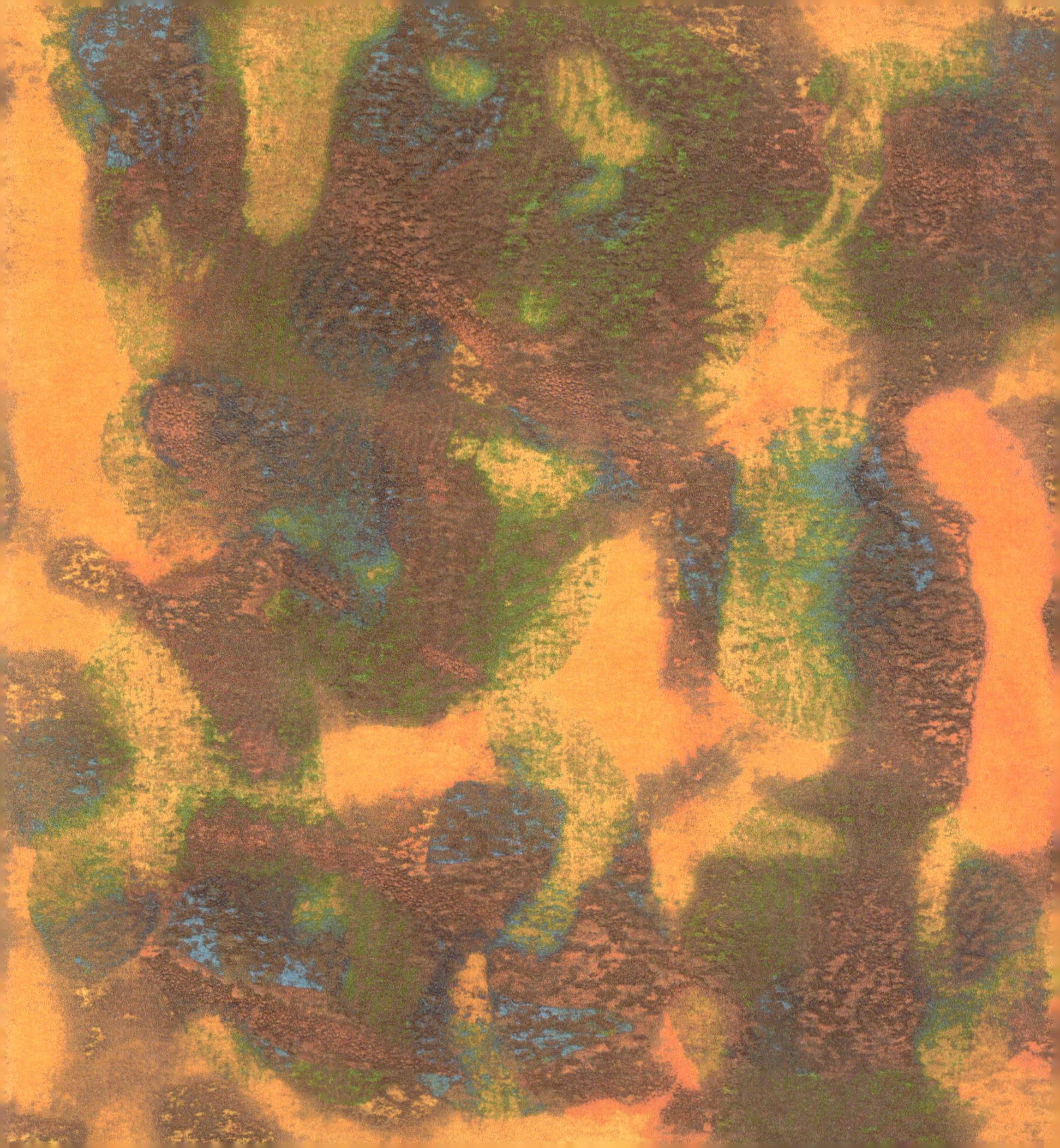

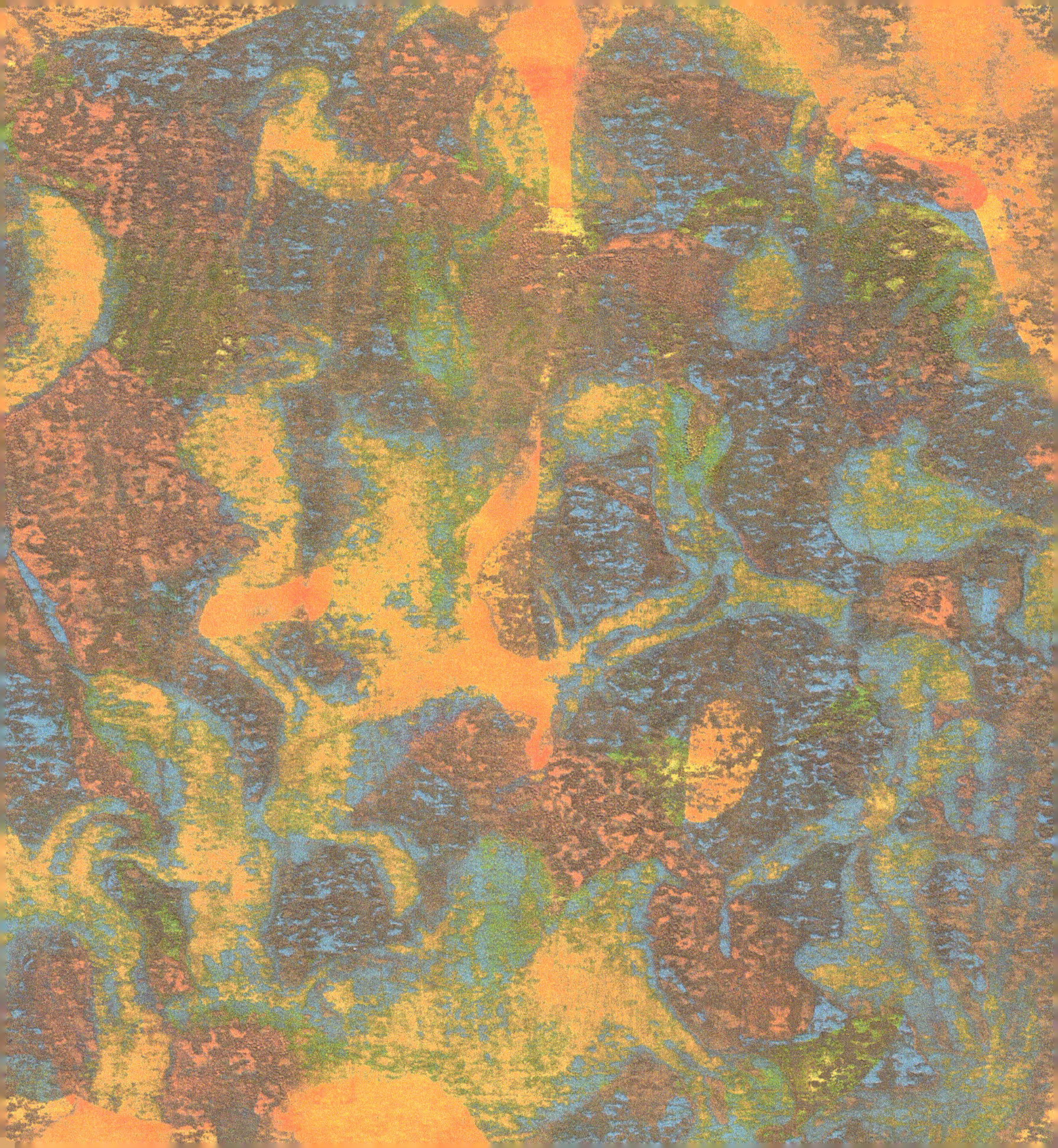

had cut earlier in the week. It must have fallen from a stalk into the sink a day earlier when I was emptying the vase of now dried-up flowers.

Despite the horror of these dismemberments I am pleased with the cats' efforts. The mice are gnawing on everything they can, including rice in the kitchen cupboards, the cupboard doors themselves, and, from the sound of it, the insulation in the ceiling above the living room. It was only a month ago, just after moving in, that I pulled a mattress out of storage in the garage to find a large hole in one end of it and a black plastic garbage bag sucked through the entire length of the mattress. Why the mice had pulled the bag into this mattress nest I don't know, or why they left it intact rather than chewed into pieces. I set up the bed, pulled a mattress pad and two sheets over the mattress, and did not tell that night's guest about what I had found.

By midnight the geese—still thousands of them, now set to overnight in this cornfield—are only somewhat quieter.

It is a day in the middle of March, and I have driven through a rainstorm and arrived home two hours before dark. At sunset I take a chair from the living room to the screen porch with a glass of cold gin. It was warm today, at least sixty degrees, but as the sun gets lower the wind picks up and the air is raw as a line of clouds brings in a new front. I have had to go back into the house twice, first for a coat and hat and then for a pair of gloves, because now the glass of gin is too cold to hold in bare hands.

I have again been brought out by the geese. It is, I think, the first time I have heard them since November. And this evening there are other birds, not the ones that I heard all winter long. Or, at least, this evening they sound different, like birds that have returned from somewhere with an ephemeral song, a tale to tell of travels. Or a song that emerges when they have just awakened. In the distance, in the valley where the cows are—and I hear them, too—there is the sound of crickets, or maybe frogs. And not just a single cricket, or frog, or locust—because now they sound like locusts, suddenly, or cicadas on a hot summer afternoon—but a swarm of whatever small creature this is. Maybe it comes from the hollow down by the creek, which probably never really froze. Within it are there frogs, or insects, that have resumed a song as if it were late summer again? Or is it some machinery, the sound of milking pumps at the dairy farm? The sound travels from left to right in the valley, and I am convinced as I listen longer that it is large and animal; suddenly I wonder if cicadas the size of barns will climb out of the valley as the nearly last red light of the sun fades.

To look away, as I have just done, can be disorienting. The sun moves that quickly: when my eyes return to where they were focused, it is no longer there. The sunlight changes much faster than anything—say, the dynamic of a cocktail party: look away, then look back; the same two people will still be talking, standing in the same place. In that same amount of time, the light of the sun on a March evening will be completely different.

The sun's angle has changed since November. This is to be expected, but, even so, it is disorienting: if I were to look now at where I would think it should be, it would not be there. In November the sun set to the south and west: south of the western mountains, over the hills and the ponds to the south. Now it is due west. In a few months, in late summer, it will set to the north and west, on the northern edge of the mountains. I will look forward to watching for the place of the sun in late summer.

At this time of day, if the clouds are just right, they will sit at the horizon, masquerading as mountains. So now, behind the hills, are distant mountains, and behind the mountains are cloud mountains, two or three times larger. I have, all of my life, squinted at clouds to take them for mountains. The first time I remember doing this was at age ten, from the back seat of a car as my family drove south outside Birmingham, Alabama, where I couldn't be sure which were the hills on the edge of a city and which were the clouds. Most people squint at clouds to find shapes within them—animals or trees, buildings, maps of countries. I have always looked for another layer of mountains, another horizon.

It is Easter, but there are no crosses on the lawns. This is unlike Christmastime, when, among the other decorations, there were strings of blue—and it was always blue—lights shaped into crucifixes. I found these decorations to be curious and misguided: a crucifix, after all, signifies death rather than birth.

What there are now, everywhere, are trees festooned with fluorescent plastic Easter eggs. This is something I had never seen until a few years ago, when on a road trip south, I spotted a few of these decorated trees along the highway in Virginia. But today, up north, they swing in the tree branches when a breeze hits them. And up here, on the hill, after the good wind that comes almost every night, Day-Glo plastic half-eggs are spread across the lawns in the morning and lie broken on the road's pavement.

It is an unusually warm day for the beginning of spring, and this has brought out animals not seen in months. My attention is drawn to a chipmunk that perches atop the woodpile at the top of the driveway, eating seed I've left out for the wild birds. I am taking in this quaint scene when a hawk swoops down from out of nowhere, snatches the chipmunk, and flies off.

Just before dark I notice the first green shoots of vegetation at the edge of the woods. On television the other night I heard that in a valley outside Las Vegas there is a yellow species of poppy that can only be found there and in a neighboring valley, but nowhere else in the world. I wonder if anything in these woods claims such singularity.

On this afternoon in June, I have just seen a film, a documentary about people who claim to have experienced alien abductions. Near the waterfall I notice two pairs of shorts laid out neatly, side by side on a rock, but there is no one there, no one swimming.

I am bathing in the waterfall when a young man slips past me at the edge of the river. He steps across the rocks upriver, then disappears into the pine woods at the other side. Soon later he emerges naked in the pool below the waterfall, having moved entirely around me in the woods. After swimming in S-turns for some time without stopping, he climbs the steep bank back up to the woods. Between the pine trunks and the underbrush, smoke emerges; then bright flashes, a white bandanna waving back and forth, the fanning of a fire. For the next twenty minutes there is blurred choreography amid the green and I can tell, even with as little as I can see, that he is still naked. When I look back a few minutes later, he is gone, the fire extinguished. I turn to the rocks behind me to catch him stepping across them once more, now clothed, and I watch as he evanesces in the woods.

I cross the rocks myself and walk through the pines, looking for where he was; I gauge the location by following with my eyes the site of where I had been sitting on the other side of the river. Coming over a small rise, I see a tiny green swamp below me, quite detached from the river, and above the swamp I find a small circle of rocks, a tiny ripple of smoke at the center of the circle. Next to it is a small igloo-shaped structure made of branches and twigs about three feet in diameter and in height. Between the fire circle and the dome is a branch, stuck in the ground at a forty-five-degree angle facing southeast. This is all I find, all I know.

❦

My hands are bruised and bleeding from pruning the thorny barberry hedge, but once again I can see the mountains from the front lawn.

❦

In the short time I've lived here I've become keenly aware of the birds in the woods. The first to really draw my attention was the wood thrush, which has an impossibly sweet and melodic song that echoes through the trees. Others I can't yet identify, so I

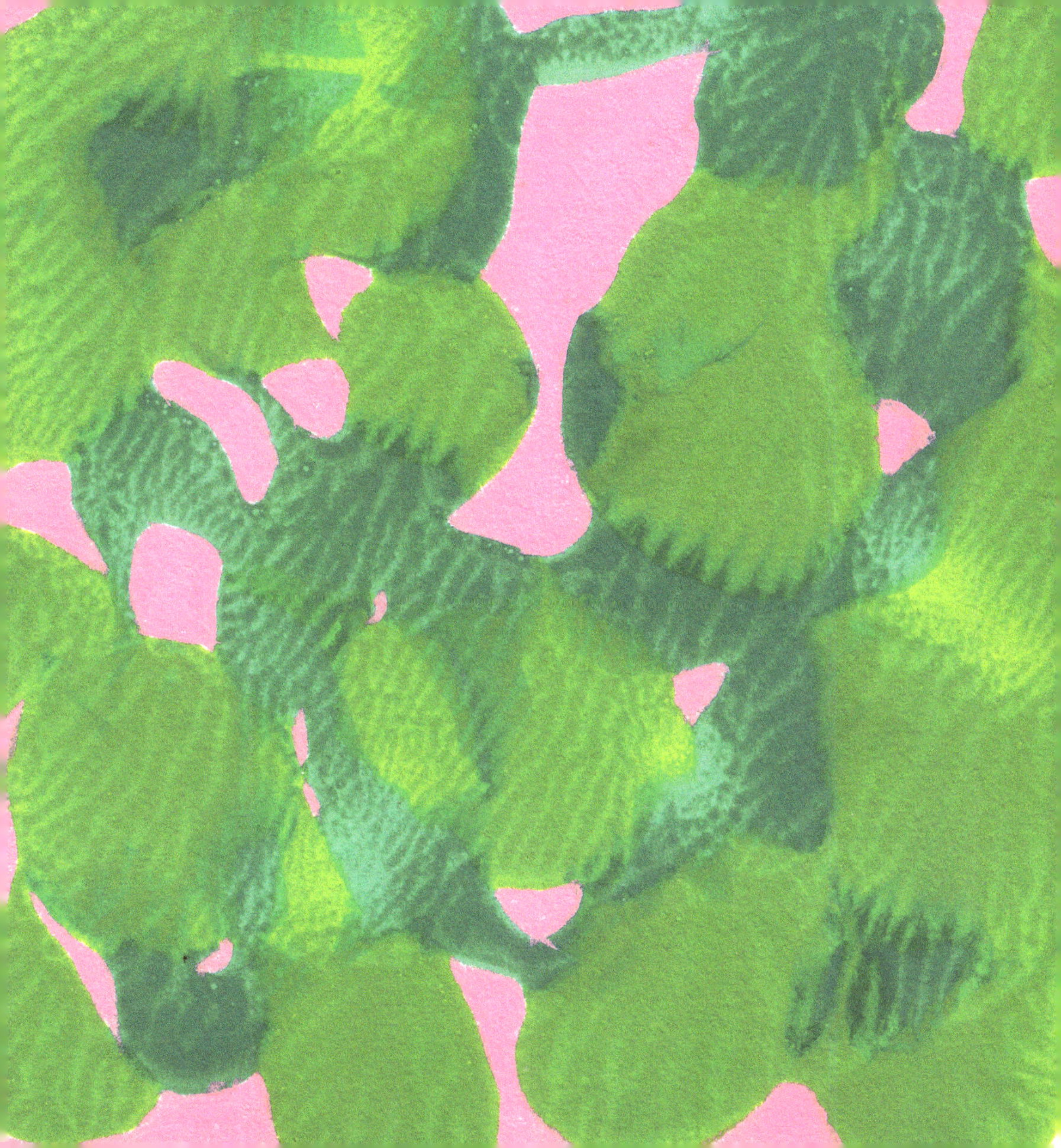

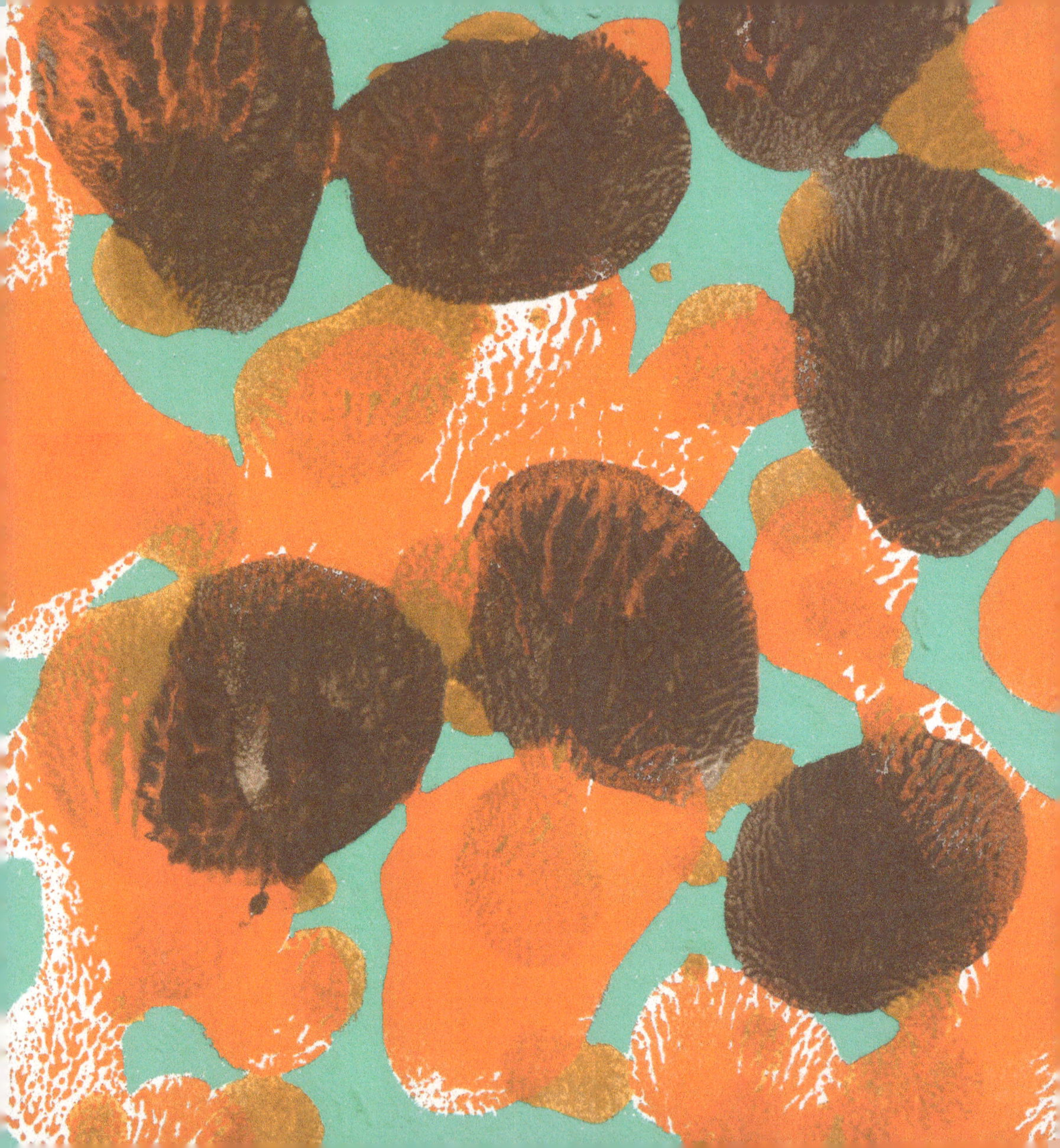

give them names based on popular culture. One of these is a bird that repeatedly calls in a seesaw sound, *HA-ha*, which reminds me of an insecure bully on a popular animated television series who always points at others and laughs—*HA-ha!*—at their misfortunes. I've named the bird Nelson, after the bully. Another has a call that sounds oddly electronic: a spiraling, downward whistle that reminds me of the famous videogame involving a character who travels through a maze and eats ghosts. The electronic spiraling sound can be heard when a video ghost dies, so I have named this one Blinky, after one of the ghosts. The last has a song that replicates exactly the opening four notes of the jazzy theme song from a decades-old television series about a private detective in Los Angeles; this is the Lalo bird, named for the composer of the theme song. It is only after some time and consultation that I find these birds are actually the black-capped chickadee, the veery, and the Baltimore oriole.

I recently met a woman who lives near here, in an old house that was once the home of the Famous Author. Ever since a biography of the Famous Author was published, in which was given the address of the house, people come by to look. Some days this woman will leave her house and be met by a small crowd on the sidewalk. And they will look at her expectantly. "Yes, it is," she tells them. "And no, you may not."

Though I might like to think I am less prying, I am only slightly so. Having never been to the woman's house, nor read the biography of the Famous Author, on my drive here I looked at mailboxes, hoping to find one that bears the last name of the woman I know. And I watched for old houses, those that look like they may have a history, like a place where the Famous Author might have lived. And I will do the same when I leave.

Now I am walking in the woods, and on cliffs, overlooking a large river. The flatness of things: How is it that this path crosses this flat gray rock, with the dimensions of a king-size bed, and so many others like it? Did someone engineer the trail this way to make use of these rocks, or is their flatness a circumstance of centuries of people treading here?

There is an old cemetery up here, at the end of the road and where the path begins. More than a hundred years of wear have made most gravestones nearly illegible: gray stubs in soil. It appears to be all one family buried here. I look for the name of the Famous Author: maybe she is here, too, maybe the lost, estranged sister, daughter, wife of someone. That this cemetery could be here, in the middle of these woods, strikes me as odd: there is no house, no church to which it could belong. There is a lake: I can see that, white-blue through the trees and lower, down a hill.

And where did the stone wall come from, layered pieces of jagged slate along so much of this path in the middle of deep woods? Was this once a road to something?

At the cliff there is a bag from a video store, and near it, in the bushes, the colored sleeve from a pornographic videotape. Beside that is the molded Styrofoam carton that contained the tape itself. Perhaps a teenager had brought it up here to unwrap it; his parents might have noticed the bulky outer packaging and bag, but the videotape alone he could slip in a coat pocket and walk in the house with.

I watch the dog run through the woods and wonder if the other, older one at home will be envious. Will he smell leaves on this dog's breath, river water air in fur?

This morning, from the top of the hill, I could see a bright, orange-yellow disk in the field across the road, perfectly round in shape, something that appeared overnight. After I summoned my two houseguests to see it, we were still uncertain of what it was, or even what it was made of—was it a Frisbee, some other plastic object, a balloon?—so binoculars were produced to quench the curiosity. What it turned out to be was a sunflower, a perfectly shaped specimen but shorter than they usually are, only about three feet tall, nestled in the tall field grass. It is, as they say, a volunteer in the unplanted, overgrown field.

I am familiar with volunteers. We were discussing them last night, as the vegetable garden is filled with volunteered tomato and pumpkin plants—the results, respectively, of the spoils of last year's tomato harvest and November's discarded jack-o'-lanterns. On the radio recently I heard a naturalist use the phrase *quite promiscuous* to refer to gourds and pumpkins; they'll hybridize with any other plants in the larger gourd family, he explained.

There were probably two hundred of the tomato seedlings, so many that I pulled them as weeds to avoid them choking out the other vegetables. Our pondering today during lunch was where the term *volunteer* comes from as relates to gardening. Are the volunteers the tomato plants that volunteered to come up this spring from the old seeds, or are they the tomatoes that volunteered last fall to rot off the plant and land in the soil?

Another volunteer came to us last night: a cat that cried from the edge of woods for an hour or more before emerging from the ferns and underbrush when one of the dogs sniffed him out. He is a green-eyed, white cat with a black tail, feet, and face and an almost perfect black circle in the middle of his stomach. These markings cause him to resemble a Holstein cow so much that I have tentatively named him Elsie, after the famous mascot for a certain brand of milk.

This was before we realized he was not female but instead a neutered male. That knowledge came to us later last night when, during an improvised trivia quiz in which we tested each other from an answer-all reference book, we came across a page on how to sex a young cat. The process is simple, based on punctuation: Raise the cat's tail. If what you see resembles a colon, it is male; if it looks like an upside-down semicolon, it is female.

I left the cat on the back porch with some food and water, and with the screen door propped slightly open should he decide to go back to where he came from. He cried for quite awhile after we turned in, then eventually quieted down. This morning I awoke to find that he was gone, and I was quite sad.

This afternoon, again on the hill in the sun, we once more heard the cry of a cat from the woods behind us, and looked up to find Elsie again volunteering himself out from the ferns and onto the lawn. He is skinny, with a backbone and ribs that are easily felt, numerous scabs and scratches against the pink skin under his white fur. The worst of these is a large, hairless and red, open wound on his tail that may be the result of walking away from a fight. He is going to stay, I would think, and will be called Elsie despite his gender—or LC, for Lucky Cat.

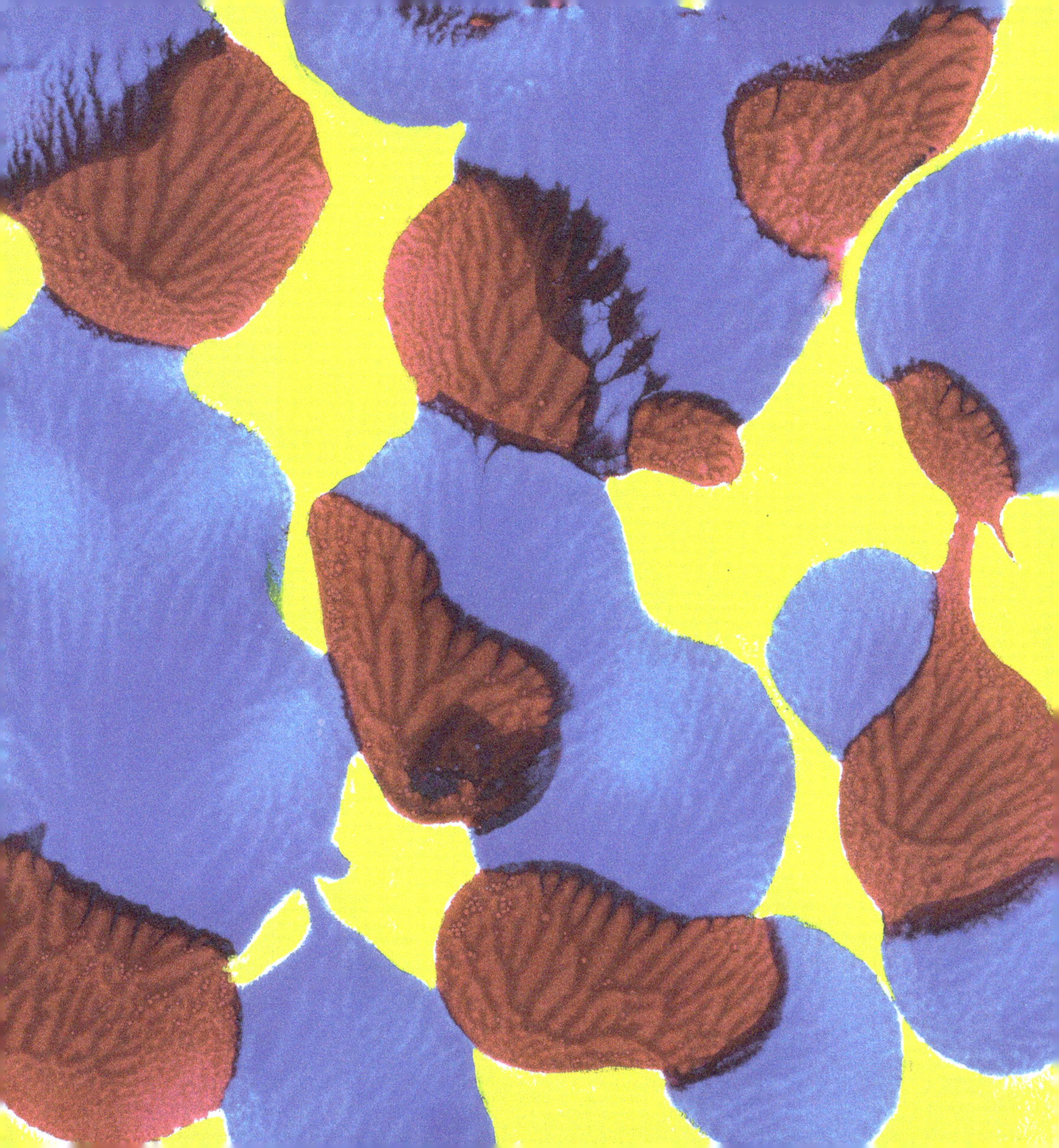

⚜

It is a humid night at the end of July. I have come out, to a blanket on the hillside, to view the shooting stars. My eyes adjust to the dark, training themselves to focus on the thousands of white lights above—or *not* focus, because it is easier to see a star if one looks slightly to the side of it rather than directly at it, having something to do with the distance between two eye and the angle of the star's light: parallax. This much I remember from junior high science classes.

Dear Diary, I could say, tonight I have seen the Big Dipper, Cassiopeia, the Milky Way, two satellites, a few airplanes, and twenty or more shooting stars. But far more exhilarating are the sounds from the hills and the woods: the shrieks of a band of coyotes, a visceral laughing that carries over from the hills more than a mile across the valley. Behind me, in the woods, one lone coyote calls in answer.

A few weeks ago a friend told me about hearing one night a band of coyotes, at close range, as they attacked and killed another animal. Instead of being horrified, she found the whole experience fascinating. It reminds you of your place in the food chain, explained my vegetarian friend.

At the edge of the yard, in tall bushes, another series of sounds builds into a low, guttural buzzing. At first I think it is my distant neighbor, talking quietly to herself, or on the phone very late at night. But as it increases in volume I hear no recognizable language, and began to think it must be a bird, or some sort of frog. I shine a flashlight in that direction, only to find nothing, and the sound dies down significantly, though not to complete silence. When I turn the light away, the buzz increases again, now louder than before. But when I aim the light back in that direction, it happens again: decrescendo. Letting the lateness and my imagination carry me, I envision a troop of small reptilian aliens just beyond the bushes at the edge of the yard, gathering their ranks in the dark spaces between the sporadic flashlight beams, advancing and retreating and advancing, a little closer each time, the buzz getting louder: *ezz ezz ezzben*—for this is the what it sounds like from here—*ezz ezz ezzben*, *ben ben ben*, *ezzben ezzben*.

I turn the flashlight away, deciding my curiosity is better left unsated—not fear, exactly, but something close to it—and retreat to the house. On the walk back, the flashlight catches the large, dark, brown form of something at the edge of the woods that startles me and demands identification: one of these aliens, a dead groundhog, a foraging raccoon? It is instead part of a dead tree felled by recent storms.

All of this causes me to wonder briefly before bedtime about other beings: when or from where they might come, or if they have already. How spiders might be aliens that came millions of years ago to trap other beings in the gluey silk hanging across every doorway and window of the house, the same webs I catch my face in almost daily. Or in the many fine, concentrically ringed webs they have spun across the wet lawn in the morning: surely these are of a higher life form.

I am visiting a friend who lives about a half hour away. She and her partner live in a small, rented house that borders a vast estate, and she often walks in the woods on the estate property, trespassing, which is what she and I are doing on this warm

September day. She takes me down a path in deep woods until we come upon an ornate cabin in a clearing. The door is not locked, so she opens it and waves me in as if it were her own home. Inside there is a beautiful, massive oak table and an ornately carved oak chair. She tells me these things have been here as long as she has been walking here—about a year, now—and that she never comes across anyone at the cabin or even in the larger woods in which it sits. She is considering stealing the chair and putting it in the living room of their small house. This is against the advisement of her partner; he is well known locally and an acquaintance of the wealthy estate owner. My friend says it would only be fair to the chair, because she is an animist, believing—as Hindus do, she points out—that even inanimate objects have a spirit, a life force. The chair is lonely here, she claims, and it needs to be sat on to fulfill its purpose in life.

When we return to the house, her partner is standing over a freshly decapitated chipmunk on the lawn; he thinks he ran over it with the mower. She tells him to dispose of it, as it is gruesome, but he refuses, giving the reasoning that their house is only a rental and it should thus not be his responsibility; he's annoyed enough that he must mow the lawn, as required by the lease. To placate my friend, I put on a glove and lift the headless rodent by its tail, intending to fling into a deep thicket of bushes where she will no longer have to look at it. But its body separates from its tail, and this throws off the trajectory: the chipmunk lands in the road, and I am left holding its tail.

Later in the evening, as I am driving away in the dark, I hear a tiny thump under the car tire and realize I have flattened what remained of the chipmunk. I am reminded of what an acquaintance once said about hitting a bird that flew into the front of his car, how he felt he had blown the life out of it. That doesn't apply here and now, of course; there is no life left to deflate. I have merely made a pancake of an already very diminished corpse.

❋ ❋ ❋

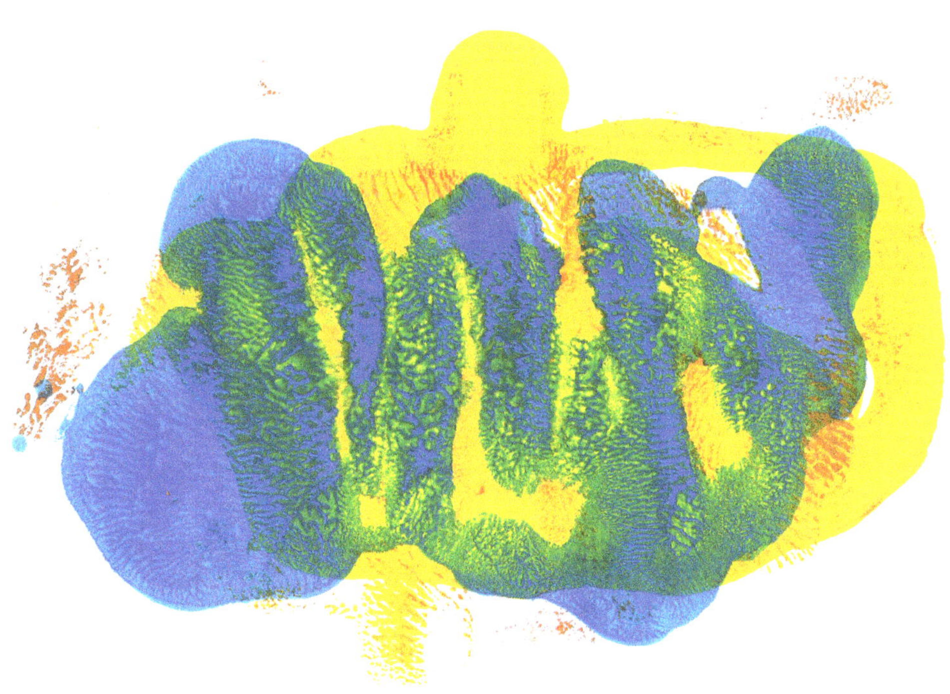

Part Two: Stolen Days

Years have passed. I am now married, and we live even deeper in the country, on a large old farm surrounded by fields, woods, and hills, on a dirt road. A creek runs through the property that can flood the fields during the spring thaw or be seared in midsummer to the point of a mere trickle. Winters are much harsher here. We say that this will be the last house either of us ever lives in.

Not long after moving here, we began keeping poultry as pets—geese, turkeys, chickens, and ducks. The first two ducks we took in, a pair of adult Muscovies given to us by a friend, were stately black-and-white birds that sported caruncles, wartlike growths, above their beaks. The caruncle was particularly prominent on the male, whom we knighted Sir Francis Drake. Then, having to come up with a suitable name for his female companion, we dubbed her Elizabeth I. In the daytime, Frank and Betty strolled around the property together like an old married couple; at dusk they made their way back to the barn to bed down in the hay.

It was not long before Betty went broody—setting, as it's called, on a clutch of nine eggs. She was a dutiful mother: for five weeks we almost never saw her leave the nest—not even to eat or drink—and we worried about her health. The last couple of weeks of this time Betty must have felt a need to stretch her wings; once a day, at about the same time every afternoon, she would emerge into the open air, fly in a mad, swooping arc around the property, and then glide straight back into the barn and onto the nest. Occasionally she would break up this tour by stopping to perch on a fencepost and survey the land around her.

During this time the otherwise docile Betty became quite unpleasant. There was never any question of checking on the eggs beneath her; if you neared the nest, Betty spread her wings,

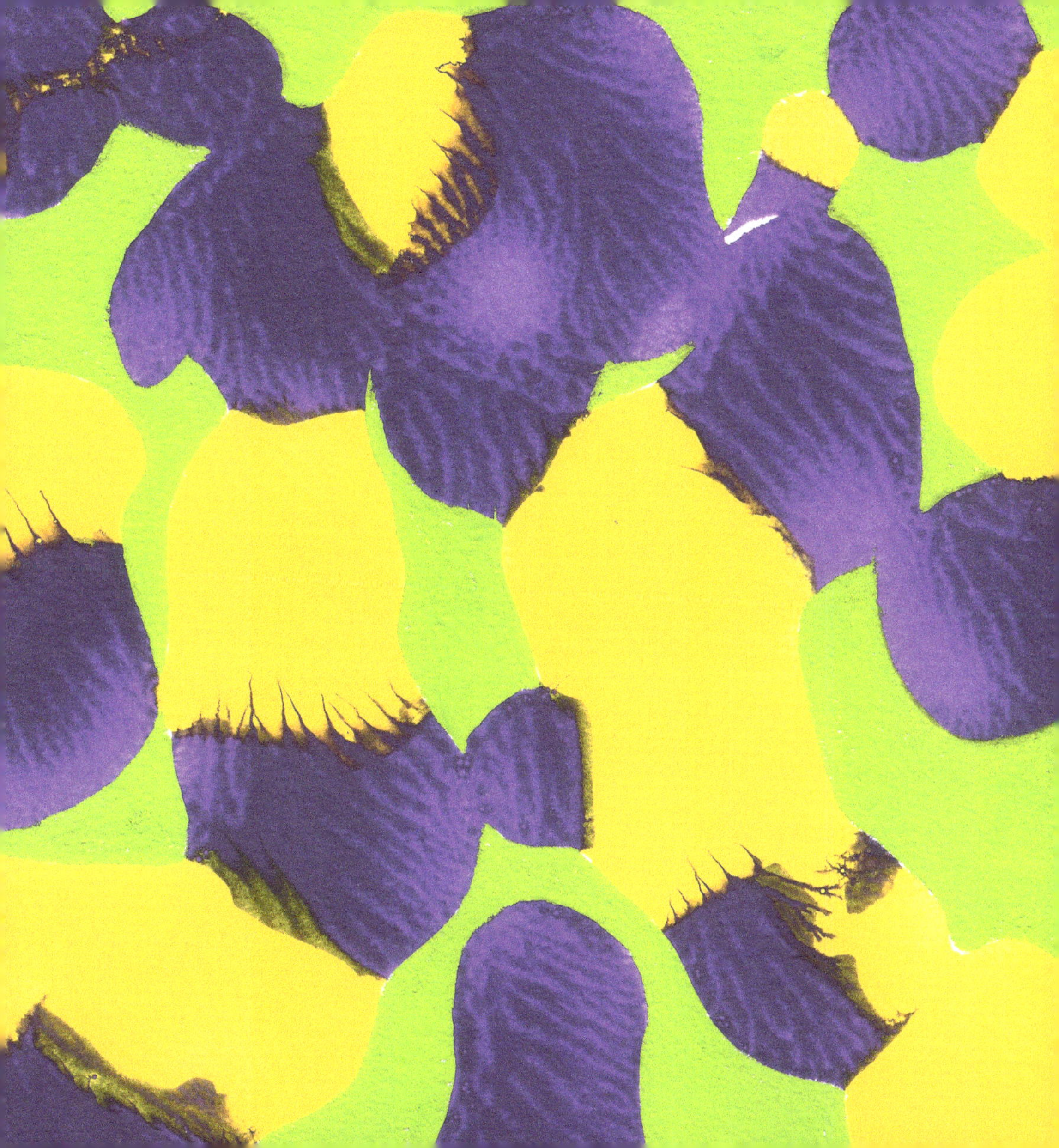

puffed herself up, and craned her neck in your direction, pecking at the air and hissing, all without rising from the hay. For these many weeks Frank was also banished from her side; he would spend most days far from the barn, lying alone in the shade of the picnic table, looking most forlorn, and he slept alone, elsewhere in the barn, at night.

Eventually Betty hatched four of the eggs and, last fall, three of the ducklings matured to look just like Frank and Betty: black and white, and with large caruncles atop their beaks, which indicated to us that they were drakes. It was impossible to tell them apart, so I named them all Darryl: Brother Darryl, Other Brother Darryl, and Another Brother Darryl, after three backwoods brothers from a well-known television sitcom some years back. The fourth duckling was female, and completely different: elegant, gray and white, looking much like a seagull. I named her Rosa, after Santa Rosa Island in the Florida panhandle, a place I've vacationed many times and where I have seen countless waterbirds.

On this late spring morning I look out the window to see Betty alarmedly circling the property. Out of the corner of my eye I catch a gray blur in the air—which I presume to be Rosa, also in flight—heading over the fields across the road. I rush outside to see what is causing all of this commotion, and I find all three Darryls on the lawn, dead and mangled. Something—likely a fox—has attacked. After circling for quite some time, Betty eventually lands in the higher branches of a tree, quite a distance down the road. I throw sticks up at it, trying to get her to leave the tree and return to our property, but she won't budge. It is at least an hour before she flies back to the barn of her own volition. After some time, Frank emerges unscathed from wherever he was hiding. Rosa is never seen again.

It is a warm evening in mid-June, and the multiflora roses are in bloom in the upper fields. Wild roses, considered undesirable and invasive, they spread not only by root but also from seed carried on the wind or by birds. A year or so after we moved here, one small multiflora rose sprouted up along the poultry fence, and I let it remain. Now, only a few years later, it is a profuse tangle of woody branches and thorns, fifteen feet across and some seven feet tall, covering an unsightly corner of the fence where nothing else has ever grown. It spreads a great deal in a short time every spring and summer, its branches ranging and curving down toward earth, where, if they reach the soil, they will set roots and start a new plant. I prune them back every year to prevent this, and to keep a pathway accessible; I have snagged clothes, hair, and even skin in the thorns. Now, with the multiflora and the rugosa bush rose I planted some years back both in peak bloom, the air everywhere is fragrant. It is a most pure scent, the absolute definition of rose.

This is one of a few sublime stretches of spring. Another came just a few weeks ago, in mid-May, when the dozen lilacs and scores of apple trees bloomed simultaneously, their fragrance coating the air, and the bright yellow marsh marigolds flowered in the creek across the road, a river of gold running through the lowlands. Still another came a few weeks after that, when the towering black locust sent out pendulous clusters of white flowers that at first smelled like orange blossoms and then—only a day later, as they aged—like jarred grape jelly. These brought out the bees, whose buzzing was an all-encompassing hum that could be heard far down the road. The locust blooms were fleeting; in a few days they fell to the lawn, where they looked like June snow, and the bees departed.

Now the bees have returned, their mass hum-buzz heard all over the roses in the daytime. At night they are silent, replaced by the bass roar of a pair of bullfrogs and the calls of green frogs, pronounced in loud, sharp gulps, in the nearby wetlands. The yard after dark is a dance hall: sound and light, frog music and the greenish-white flickering lamps of thousands of fireflies, gliding through the tall grass and over the fields, rising and spinning into the sky's stars, a giant blinking disco ball.

In a pen up in the barn, a chicken has been sitting on a nest for many weeks—more time than it should take to hatch the eggs underneath her. This morning my partner asks me if I think she's all right, and I answer that I checked on her recently and seem to remember that she shifted her head to glare in my direction, protective of her clutch of eggs. Even so, I decide to look in on her, and when I near the nest she doesn't stir or even raise her head. Moving closer, I nudge her gently with my foot, and she flops over on her side, stiff as a board. Upon closer examination I notice that the hen has been dead so long that a thick layer of dust has collected on her back.

We live in a bowl.

This is the decision I've come to on this warm, clear night in August as I stand in the yard and stare up at the skies. Our house is in a clearing, surrounded by the high hills and woods that make up the rest of our land and that of our immediate neighbors. Everything this night—the trees at the rim of the bowl, and the stars—is circular and swirling above and around me.

Last fall we bought Indian runner ducks: tall, slender wine-bottle birds that stand upright and cannot fly but do, in fact, run everywhere, as their name implies—usually en masse, as they have a bit of a herd mentality, and with a lot of quacking. They are comical birds, at times a bit clumsy. They are also prolific layers of large, green-shelled eggs, but they are useless at hatching them because they never sit on them. Sometimes a female runner will be running across the poultry pen when an egg will simply pop out of her rear end; she will continue on her way, seemingly none the wiser, and the egg will just lie there in the dirt.

Because we know that Betty the Muscovy will dutifully sit on a nest up in the barn, we slipped some runner duck eggs under her in the spring. They hatched about a month ago, and now we have two sets of runners, one in a pen in the barn and another in the larger poultry pen nearer to the house.

Every morning I've taken to letting Betty and her seven ducklings out of the barn for a supervised walk around the yard. I am not the only guardian on these walks; Hazel, a grand and matronly buff-colored goose who also sleeps in the barn at night, has likewise designated herself a responsible party. While Betty leads the ducklings, much like a drum major at the head of a poorly organized marching band, Hazel brings up the rear. When Hazel and I steer them back to the barn, she knows to stop where the ducklings cross the threshold of their pen. If Hazel forgets herself, Betty, who is half her size, will remind her. She is content to have the goose as an escort, but if Hazel gets near the pen—or even, for that matter, too close to the ducklings during their outdoor strolls—Betty will turn with a loud quack and peck her back into position. This has been the routine every morning for weeks, but I never cease to marvel at it.

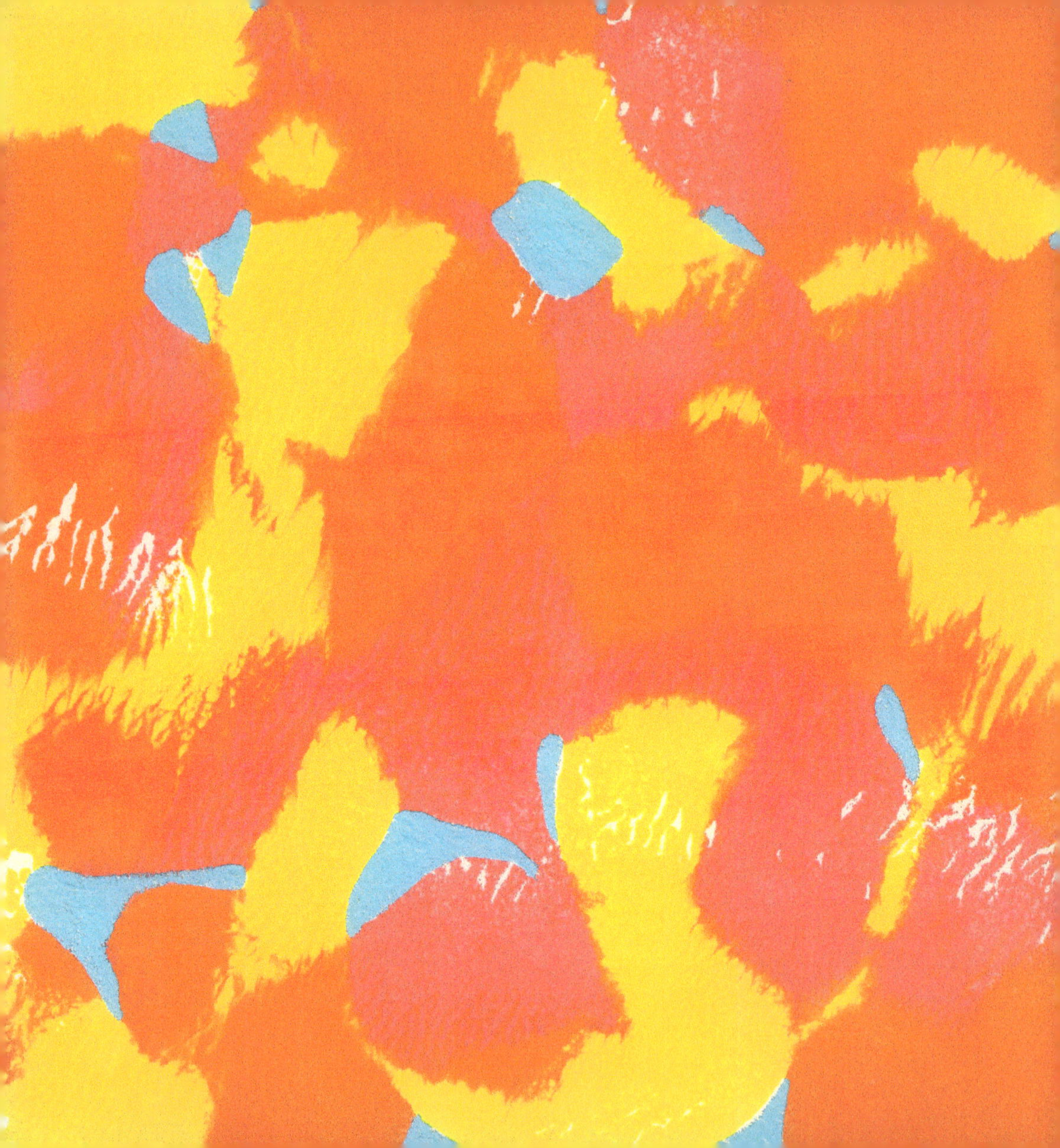

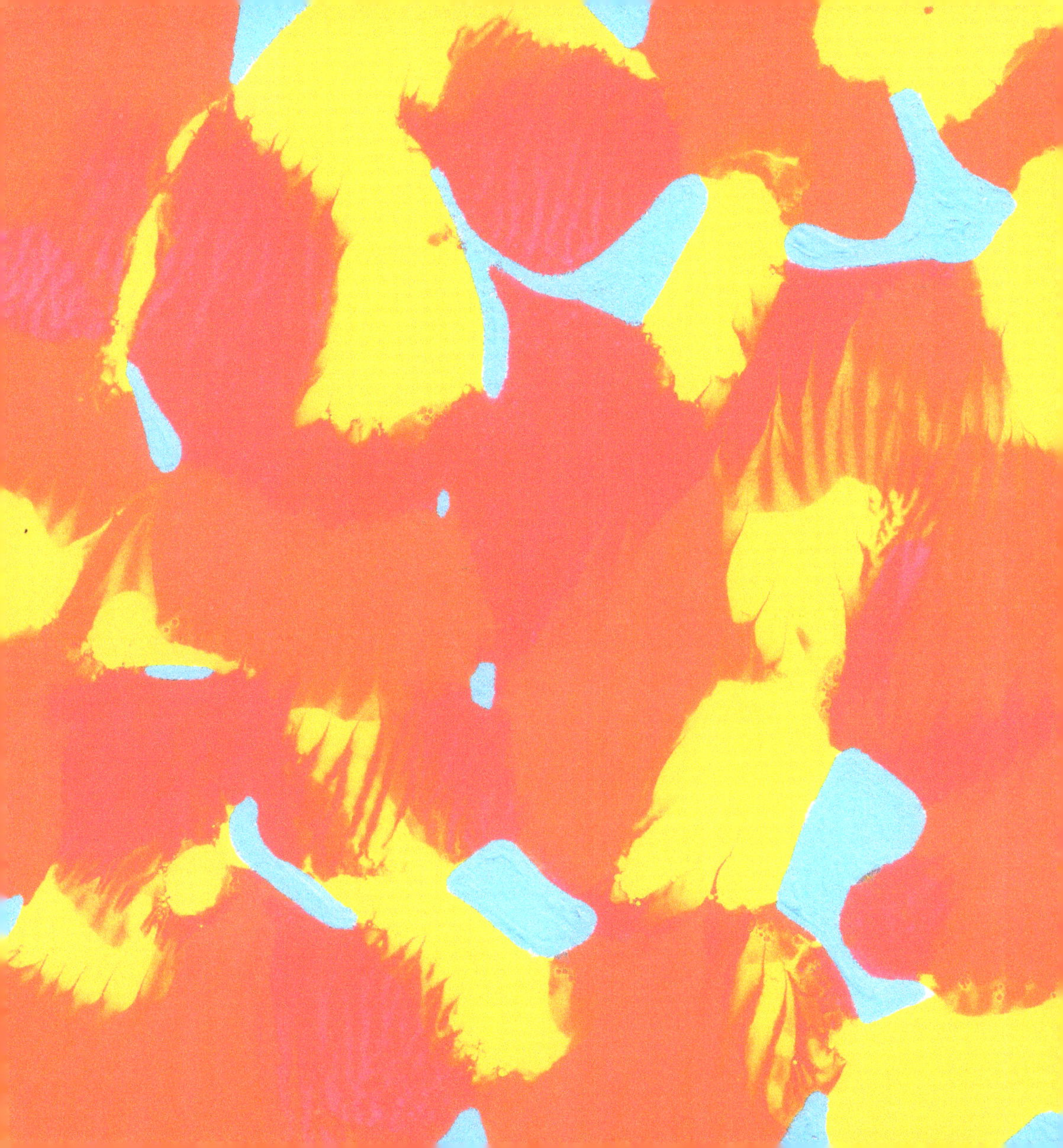

⁂

It is early autumn. We have lost to predators all but one of the seven runner ducks hatched in the barn this spring. This summer we also lost Frank, the Muscovy drake, to old age. I have decided that it is time to move the one surviving runner duck, a beautiful chocolate-brown female, from the barn to the poultry pen, where there are five other runners.

It does not go well. The other ducks are not as welcoming as I had imagined they'd be, and the two male runners are especially brutal toward the young one; she is repeatedly chased, mounted, and pecked. Usually birds resolve these squabbles on their own, so I leave them to sort it out.

By evening I see no sign of her, so I head outside. I find the brown duck in a corner of the pen, her head stuck in a tight section of the wire fence, motionless. I think she is dead, but as I reach to pick her up she quacks and struggles. It takes me a half minute to free her from the fence, and I realize she will be better off back in the barn with Betty the Muscovy and Hazel the goose.

I begin to carry her toward the barn, but the brown duck protests, flapping her wings and squawking, so I set her down to walk on her own, walking behind her to steer her in the right direction. She walks a few feet, then plops down in the grass. She is exhausted. I nudge her, but she looks up, directly at me, and lets out a gentle, plaintive quack, as if to say, I'm very tired; could you carry me? I am riddled with guilt for having put her through the earlier trauma, and as I bend to pick her up I expect she will fuss again, but this time she is quiet and subdued, content to be carried the rest of the way to the barn.

The brown duck rallies when she sees Betty, who is in turn ecstatic. Both ducks bob their heads up and down in greeting, and Betty issues her into the pen. Betty beds down, and the brown runner slips under her wing and falls asleep. I decide that this duck needs a name. I do some research and find that Queen Elizabeth I, Betty's namesake, had a lady of the bedchamber and close companion named Katherine Astley. From now on the brown duck will be Katherine.

Another winter has come, and yesterday evening we had rain on top of the foot or snow of snow that fell earlier this week; the temperature dropped at the same time, and the rain built up in a thick layer of ice.

This morning, when I open their coop door, the Indian runner ducks run out, as they are always wont to do, and immediately hit the crust of ice on the gentle slope. All five skate, en masse and uncontrollably, from one end of the pen to the other—a distance of about fifty feet. This causes me to laugh, but all turns sour very quickly when I realize that, with their flat, webbed feet and very low body mass, the ducks have no traction whatsoever. They are sliding all over the ice, flailing. I have to pick them up and carry them back up to a level area, as they are exhausting themselves trying to gain traction. There is a very real danger of them twisting their legs, and while ducks usually recover from lameness (though it can take weeks), there's nothing sadder than a lame, limping duck.

The chickens—who, despite having claws—go through the same graceless ice dance. Most just give up and return to their coop. I spend a half hour breaking up the ice with a garden rake—raking paths all over the garden—and then spread hay to give added traction.

The turkeys are much heavier, and have huge talons, so they fare nominally better. The geese, despite their massive weight, are like the ducks: their webbed feet completely give out from under them and their legs splay on the ice. I issue them back to their coop, and they show no interest in venturing out again, despite my having broken pathways through the ice. That's probably for the best.

On a warm night in late April, the wetlands between our place and our neighbors' farm to the south ring out with evensong. This began, weeks ago, with the spring peepers, aptly named chorus frogs: just a few at first, then more each successive night; now there are thousands, ringing like chimes. As the sky grows darker, wood frogs add their series of ratcheting, grinding *chacks*. Over all of this the American toads sing sustained trills, and two Wilson's snipes—wading birds that migrate through for a few weeks this time of year—catch wind in their tail feathers, winnowing a ghostlike *hu-woo-woo-woo* as they circle over the wetlands. It is deafening; the overtones ring in my ears, an almost hallucinogenic tinnitus.

And it is otherworldly: I am reminded of the ominous keening of unseen aliens approaching in old science fiction movies, pulsing and swelling, louder still as night settles in.

We have, sadly, become accustomed to the death of poultry. Sometimes it comes at the jaws of foxes, raccoons, fishers, or coyotes. Such murders can at least be rationalized as part of the food chain: these mammals, too, must eat. A patch of feathers on the lawn is often the only evidence; the dead bird has been dragged back to a den somewhere to feed a predator's young. Other times there is no sign at all; birds simply disappear.

Other times illness brings death, but we have had a few successes, nursing sickly chickens back to health in dog crates in the house. We took a beloved docile rooster with a leg infection to a veterinarian to have the necrotic tissue cut away, then applied salves and wraps to his legs for weeks until he was walking nimbly and crowing again. But the rooster was old, and as fate would have it, he died a week after his recovery.

The pecking order is ruthless in chickens: if they detect sickness or weakness in another, they will mercilessly peck at it and batter it around. Ducks do not generally share this trait. One morning recently we found an old Indian runner duck dead on the lawn. The other runners were gathered around her, gently nudging her with their beaks to awaken her. When the dead duck didn't respond, they all lay down next to her, as if holding a wake. They only finally dispersed—and, even then, reluctantly—when the dead duck was taken away.

Not all is so dour. Betty the Muscovy has hatched another clutch of runner duck eggs—eleven of the thirteen I put under her, an astounding rate of success. Uncharacteristically, she allowed Katherine, the chocolate-brown runner who is her constant companion and ersatz daughter, to remain with her for the many weeks of brooding. Katherine slept on Betty's back the whole time, and the ducklings have now imprinted on both of them as mothers.

On this hot July day, I am out driving, not far from a village named Index, when I spot a street sign reading KUKENBERGER MEADOW LA., and this gets me to thinking about road signs I have seen in years of travels: HOGSBACK RD.; LAKE FIVE RD.; SCISM RD.; BUTTS CROSSING and BUTTS HOLLOW RD.; SQUIRREL LEVEL RD. (site of a Civil War battle); STEVE'S CHEESE RD.; the impossibly named BRUCE PORN LA.; the corner of CHURCH and INCINERATOR.

Kukenberger Meadow Lane, I quickly discover, is not an actual road but a long driveway—undoubtedly that of the Kukenbergers. This is common in rural areas: buying a personalized street sign that looks like a real one and naming your long driveway. Sometimes these signs reflect particular pastimes or affections: NASCAR TRAIL, JOHN DEERE HWY., BUDWEISER BLVD.; other times they are the names of a family, as in KUKENBERGER MEADOW LA., or a beloved daughter, as in HEATHER LEIGH LA. Such naming, of course, often leads those out for a country drive to turn onto these roads, if for no reason other than a photo op. Often this results in the original sign poster adding another sign later on to fend off unwanted traffic: PRIVATE DRIVE.

I am reminded of signs that go up to name places for what they destroy. Someone I know once lived in a suburban development named Laurel Oaks, where hundreds of acres of laurel oak trees were cut down to make room for the houses. And years back, when I lived in a city, a new condominium tower was named Pear Tree Place because of the majestic pear tree that towered over the sidewalk in front of it. The new high-rise building blocked sunshine to the tree, and after only a few years it died.

It is mid-November, and overnight we had our first appreciable snowfall, mixed with freezing rain, coating everything in slush and ice. The large white pine next to the poultry pen is particularly dispirited, its iced branches hanging very low. I must walk around rather than under it, careful not to brush up against it; pine branches are fragile on the best of days, more so when coated in ice.

We have had a long, mild autumn up to now: many days with warm temperatures. They are stolen days: stolen from summer or from winter, depending on how one sees it, or stolen from time as one grows older. We have still not had a killing freeze; a series of minor frosts did in most of the vegetable garden weeks ago, but the kale, chard, beets, and celery are still alive, if not exactly thriving.

As are the snapdragons: a deep green, color amid every other brown thing in the flower beds. But this morning they are coated in a layer of ice, sagging like the white pine. And, as I do with the pine, I walk around them during my morning chores, skirting them so as not to break their iced stems as I carry pails to the faucet on the side of the house for poultry water.

The snapdragons still have buds, and I am trying to protect them should they decide, on some warm day in the near future, to bloom again. I must disabuse myself of this optimism.

It is midnight in the middle of March, and we have had an uncharacteristically warm spread of a few days. Heading out with the dogs to gather logs from the woodshed, I grab a flashlight, but once outside I realize I don't need it.

How bright it is: I can make out every tree, the sheds near the house, and every slope of the immediate landscape, all of it tinted a pale and smoky blue. Looking up, I see the full moon—in

March, the Worm Moon—surrounded by a series of rings that range from pale yellow at the center to slate blue at the outer edges. The air is thick with moisture, and the moon has lit the fog. I can smell the soil for the first time in months; in the field I can hear the buzzing *meep* of a woodcock, one of the earliest birds to arrive each spring.

But the blue of this landscape is not the only surprising thing. Somehow the combination of fog and moonlight have given the illusion that everything is in miniature: the potting shed and woodshed, the garden gate, the maple trees that tower four stories overhead, the car in the driveway. A shrunken landscape: a doll's land, an HO train set on a tabletop, the realm of a garden gnome.

Everything in miniature. Everywhere blue fog. And, if it can be said, the opposite of shadow.

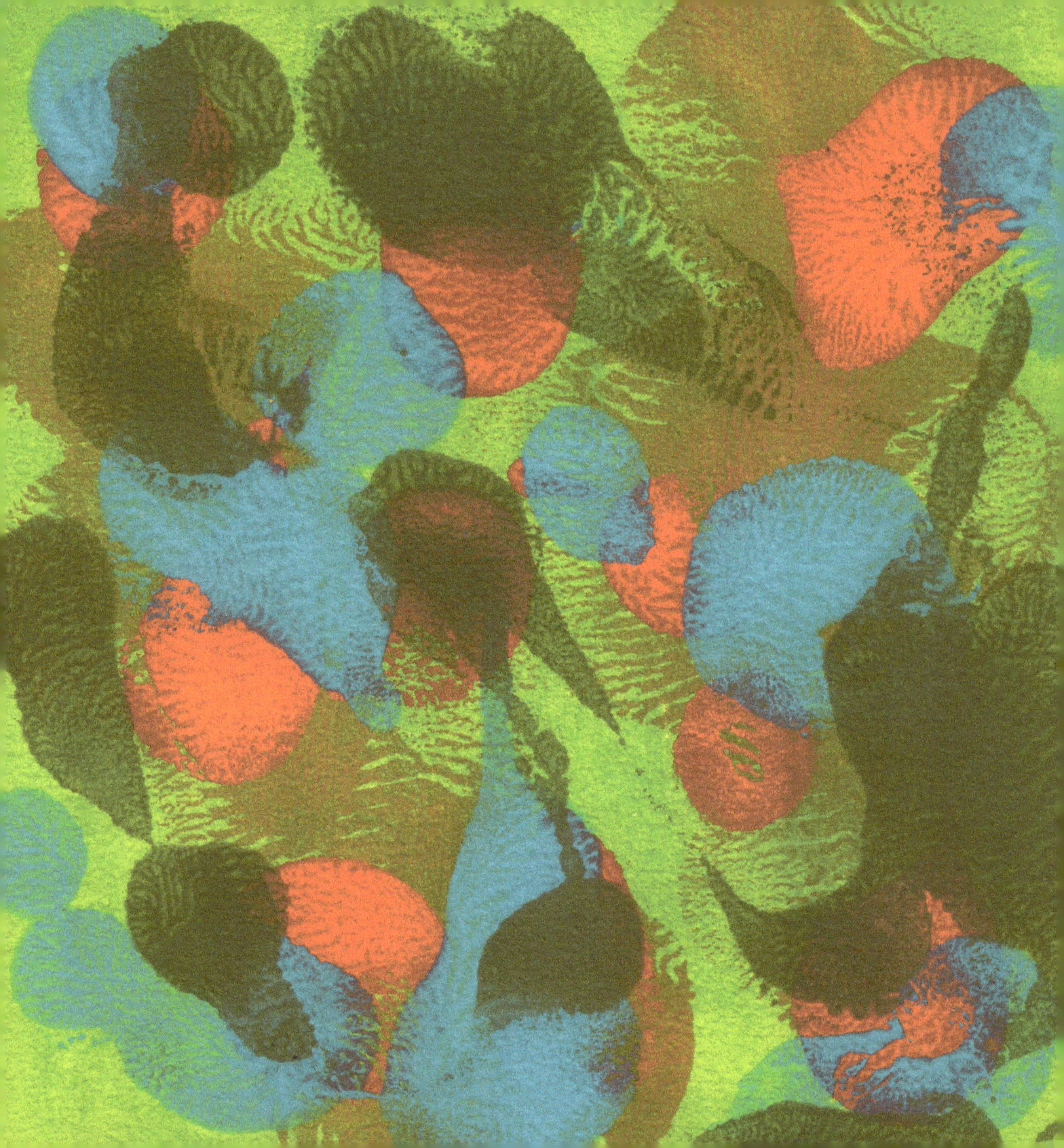

Linda Smith began making music in Baltimore during the early 1980s with various bands. Following a move to New York City in 1984, she formed the Woods with Brian Bendlin, Peggy Bitzer, and Steven Cheslik-DeMeyer. After purchasing a four-track cassette machine during that time, Linda began to record her songs at home; from 1987 to 2001 she released music on such labels as Harriet, Feel Good All Over, Slumberland, Shrimper, and her own Preference label. In 2021 Captured Tracks released a vinyl collection of her home recordings titled *Till Another Time*. Since then she has returned to recording new music, with *Untitled 1-10 Plus 1* (Almost Halloween Time Records), and *A Passing Cloud*, a collaboration with Nancy Andrews (Grapefruit/Gertrude). She received an MFA in visual art from Vermont College of Fine Art in 2008.

Brian Bendlin moved to New York City from the Midwest in the 1980s. He was the first drummer for the band Crash, and has been a drummer and percussionist in numerous other bands and ensembles, including Robin Crutchfield's Dark Day, Nothing But Happiness, the Joan Group, and the Balinese gamelans Chandra Kanchana and Giri Mekar. After the breakup of the Woods in 1986, Brian and Steven Cheslik-DeMeyer released a series of DIY solo and collaborative cassette albums in the late 1980s under the catchall banner Trouble Picnic, including Brian's ambient album *13 Groves* (1987); they also formed the acoustic trio Two Houses (with Lloyd Miller), which played live in New York, London, and Berlin in 1988. Brian received an MFA in writing from Bard College in 1996; he now lives on a farm in upstate New York with his partner Robert McBrien and a lot of animals.

Linda and Brian have been friends and collaborators for almost forty years. An album of mid-1980s tracks by their band the Woods, *So Long Before Now*, will be released on Dot Matrix / Modern Harmonic in 2023. They would like to thank Dennis Callaci for coming up with the idea of this book collaboration and for rereleasing *13 Groves* on CD, as well as Mark Givens for his exquisite book design.

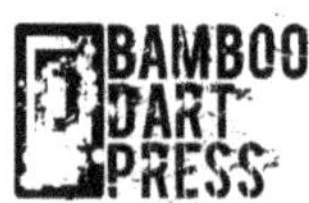

112 N. Harvard Ave. #65
Claremont, CA 91711

chapbooks@bamboodartpress.com

www.bamboodartpress.com

www.ingramcontent.com/pod-product-compliance
Lightning Source LLC
LaVergne TN
LVHW060628110826
845147LV00015B/960

* 9 7 8 1 9 4 7 2 4 0 8 6 5 *